IN SEARCH OF DOCTOR WATSON

A Sherlockian Investigation

MOLLY CARR

Paperback ISBN 978-1-78092-031-3
ePub ISBN 978-1-78092-032-0
PDF ISBN 978-1-78092-033-7

Published in the UK by MX Publishing
335 Princess Park Manor, Royal Drive, London, N11 3GX
www.mxpublishing.co.uk
Cover design by www.staunch.com

Contents

Acknowledgement

I would like to thank Roger Johnson of The Sherlock Holmes Society of London, Editor of The Society's Journal and a fount of knowledge about, among many other interests, all things to do with Sherlock Holmes and his friend and Colleague in fighting crime, the incomparable Doctor John H. Watson, for reading this book and making so many valuable suggestions, most of which I have adopted. Any shortcomings which remain are, of course, my own.

Introduction

There are several ways in which one can search for Doctor Watson, or indeed any fictional character of sufficient interest to a large enough number of readers. But the main way is through the information given about him by Sir Arthur Conan Doyle. This can be both amplified and commented on. However, there is also the use made by others of the character as a Watson, or someone very like him.

This is what I have tried to do in this book; so that it falls naturally into two parts: the Doctor as written about by Doyle, and an exploration of the concept of the foil before, during and after the first appearance of Watson. How successful have other authors been with *their* Watsons, both male and female? And how successful are the tales which, sometimes bearing little or no relation to the original, nevertheless continue to be written because the character (and the detective he admires so much) has acquired a life of its own? This, in my opinion and that of others, has the potential to make anything new as interesting as the canonical investigations: or perhaps even more interesting to those who like their heroes' adventures brought up to date.

But, according to P. N. Furbank in volume seven ('The Modern Age') of *The Pelican Guide to English Literature* edited by Boris Ford, in seeking to modernise him the status of the hero has sunk. Violent and treacherous criminals can only be defeated by a corresponding amount of violence and treachery. The reader, while theoretically remaining on the side of law, virtue and patriotism, is able to enjoy the criminal life to the full. An exception to this is Sapper's hero Bulldog Drummond, an active, courageous and honourable Edwardian gentleman who defends himself with his fists as befits his code. According to Furbank he can, on occasion, show unexpected mental resources as well: making him "a mixture of Holmes and Watson". But, again according to Furbank, in the newer thriller the moral issue is of little account. The hero is no longer a gentleman but "an efficient and savage animal, with gleaming teeth, lean body and narrow hips; an anonymous engine for detection, murder, fornication, the driving of fast automobiles and the consumption of branded goods."

One of the great charms of the Holmes-Watson tales is that in recreating them as they were, or as nearly as we can make them to what they were, we experience a kind of longing, a nostalgia for something which, according to Michael Holroyd in a B.B.C. Radio 4 broadcast, we never really had: a straining after an earlier era which, rightly or wrongly, is now seen as less stressful, less frantic and less frightening. Perhaps that's why television's latest attempt to drag Doyle into the twenty-first century by providing Sherlock Holmes with mobile phones, high-powered microscopes and the ability to send text messages has met with such a mixed reception from so many ardent fans.

But according to Alan Bradley, in an interview for New Books, detective fiction has moved out of the drawing room into the gutters and back alleys of large cities, and in so doing shifted from humanity to technology. However, it is still the case that 'The tension between the act of murder and its setting is paramount. Sudden death in a rubbish bin is hardly surprising, while some unpleasant character, bumped off during an English village's festival of carols, seems bursting with colourful possibilities'.

Sudden death in any kind of bin wouldn't suit Doyle's style at all. He rarely offends against middle-class mores, or gives too distressing a picture of the times. He wouldn't, for example, let 'The Cardboard Box' be published as part of a book after it appeared in *The Strand Magazine*. It was "too shocking".

Richard Lancelyn Green, in his introduction to *The Oxford Sherlock Holmes*, says that Doyle was adept at promoting his own work. A promotion also evident in the text of his tales. Most of Holmes' *Adventures* include one or more references to the other investigations. Doyle also paid to advertise Sherlock in a number of newspapers. Are these perhaps two of the many reasons why this particular detective became so much part of the National Psyche?

To T.S. Eliot, in a review in *The Criterion* for April 1929, the greatest of all the Sherlock Holmes mysteries is that 'When we talk of him we invariably fall into the fancy of his existence'. This reality was a quality which from the beginning 'struck readers and critics alike'. From fiction the Great Detective became, in the minds of his readers, non-fiction. Along with his willing companion. So, in the opening chapters of *this* tale, we go with Watson to university, follow in his footsteps to the Royal Military Hospital at Netley where he trains to be an army surgeon, help him decide which regiment he should be in and how to find his brigade, sympathise with him when he is struck down by enteric fever, supposedly in Peshawar, and see him safely to London and his momentous meeting through the agency of 'young Stamford' with the only consulting detective in the world. Someone whose name figures in no newspaper and who claims no official credit for solving crimes.

We later meet the Doctor as friend, companion and chronicler and discover he is a fine literary historian, as well as an enthusiastic traveller. He is also fond of music, particularly 'scotch airs', and the German composer Mendelssohn. He knows something about art, thinks Sherlock doesn't and is then contradicted by him. But, unlike Holmes, Watson cannot dismiss an investigation from his mind while it is still in progress. He is also quite incapable of keeping a secret.

The ex-army man can be found, very thinly disguised, in Agatha Christie; and his appearance in the media dates from the earliest invention of radio, television and film. In addition to all this, Watson's writings have been an endless source of interest for those determined to sort out the chronology of his adventures, the date and number of his marriages, where he went to school and even what he had for breakfast – and where he had it.

We can marvel at the liberties taken with Doyle's text in order to fit a theory: and watch some writers quarrel with the author's own description of Watson to the extent that, although when he first arrives on the scene he is still in his twenties and said to be "as thin as a lath", (and later so good-looking that Holmes says he has natural advantages with women), he is often portrayed as middle-aged, large, ugly – and looking more like a Prussian bully than an English gentleman.

Sherlock Holmes wasn't given much of a biography by Doyle, and there is a sense in which he doesn't need one. His all-absorbing interest in crime makes him slightly inhuman and something of a cipher. Wherever he wanders, his base is always Baker Street and he stays there even after Watson leaves, presumably now able to pay the rent without the assistance of a fellow lodger. Watson has written up many of the investigations for the editor of a new magazine and will continue to do so, bringing that little bit of extra fame which must increase the number of

Sherlock's cases and presumably his bank balance. This despite Holmes' insistence that the work is its own reward - though he makes a notable exception when dealing with the Duke of Holdernesse in the enquiry known as 'The Priory School'.

But apart from the scant information the Detective gives about his ancestry – his forebears were "country squires" and he had a French grandmother – there is little to build on if one wishes to write a half-ways true story of his life. Why, he doesn't even divulge enough for us to discover with any certainty which university he went to, Oxford or Cambridge!

Later writers can indulge their imaginations by giving him a wife, children, grandchildren or whatever else they fancy. They can involve him in adventures with the famous and the infamous, the living or the dead, the real and the unreal. They can turn him into a 'Doctor Who' figure as in the latest BBC television series, or make him a champion pugilist in the latest action-packed film. A film which pushes his intellectual prowess into the background. One or other of us will swallow anything, whole. But perhaps there is a kind of inevitability in the more high-profile protagonist in a series becoming the main focus of attention; although a book by Joseph Green and Peter Ridgeway Watt published in 2007 (*Alas Poor Sherlock –the Imperfections of the World's Greatest Detective*, to say Nothing of his Medical Friend), doesn't forget to include Watson. However, according to Mark Campbell in *Sherlock Holmes* (Pocket Essentials, 2007), "A good way to measure the appeal of any fictional character is to see how many imitations it spawns." This, as he says, would make Sherlock Holmes very popular indeed. He was imitated very early on by J. M. Barrie, and even Doyle himself who wrote a parody ('The Field Bazaar') for an Edinburgh University magazine, *The Student*, less than ten years after the publication of *A Study in Scarlet*. In addition to this, the period between 1896 and 1920 saw hundreds of attempts to copy Doyle's most widely known creation. Since then, Sherlock has been involved with Dracula and Frankenstein (two characters which attract as much attention as himself judging by the number of times they are parodied), met with aliens from outer space, used to solve real-life crimes and paired with several famous real-life people such as Sigmund Freud and Bertrand Russell. In *The Last Sherlock Holmes Story*, labelled 'tasteless' by Owen Dudley Edwards in his book *The Quest for Sherlock Holmes*, Michael Dibden has the Great Detective crossing swords with Jack the Ripper. Other authors with the same idea produced their own books, which include Robert Weverka's *Murder by Decree* and E. B. Hanna's *The Whitechapel Horrors.*

When considering a life story, however, Watson has both too little and too much biography; and what is there is so muddled and mistaken that it becomes something of a marathon to sort it all out. In addition, Doyle gives the supposed Doctor so little to do in the medical line that one could be forgiven for thinking he might have been a ward orderly at Netley sharp enough to pick up sufficient knowledge from the doctors surrounding him to pass himself off as an ex-army surgeon (who, however, had never been near Afghanistan) and that his later 'Practices' consisted mainly in providing nostrums for rich old women with imaginary illnesses. This subversive theory would receive a set-back when Watson met "Your old schoolfellow, Percy Phelps" during the investigation into a stolen Naval Treaty. And, before that, his dresser recognises him as his former boss at Bart's.

There would also be the wounded shoulder and the "tropical" tan to account for. But none of these hurdles stopped 'Sagittarius' [Olga Katzin-Miller] from questioning the Doctor's credentials in *The London Mystery Magazine,* where she writes:

> Holmes left one unsolved mystery,
> The case of the strange M.D.;
> Was he ever qualified?/
> Had he anything to hide?
> And why was he always free?
> Facts of his previous history
> Researchers fail to trace,
> But there's something queer in his medical career,
> For he never had a single case!"

This last line, of course, is an example of poetic licence. Watson treated Vincent Hatherley for quite a serious wound in 'The Engineer's Thumb', and says he sometimes saw injured railwaymen in his surgery. But it is interesting to note that he was being presented as bogus over sixty years ago.

However, it emerges that the Watson character is technically no less important than Holmes. The French writer Pierre Nordon, in his book *Conan Doyle* published in translation in 1966 by John Murray, says that as a companion and a witness to Sherlock's powers of detection the Doctor is the very incarnation of *vox populi,* making him democratic and thus very popular abroad. He has both psychological and literary significance. And, according to Ian Sinclair in his 2001 Introduction to the Penguin Classics Edition of *A Study in Scarlet,* Watson was invented to invent Holmes. He is a "provincial" innocent enough to do justice to the Holmes legend, and provides the framework within which Holmes can demonstrate his genius.

The Doctor regards the Detective's deductions as almost miraculous until they are explained to him. He is, therefore, often behind the readers, who may already have some inkling of what is to be revealed later and can thus feel very superior. As a result of this feeling, they will always be on Holmes' side – even at his most maddeningly secretive. The Detective knows all, will eventually tell all, and the readers are (for the most part) up there with him. Watson is around to ask questions as the story progresses, which is a great help. He does this even when Holmes is not present, resting his wounded leg and soliloquising among the newspapers as he tries to work out the various puzzles presented to him.

On a more domestic level Terry Manners, in his book about Jeremy Brett published by Virgin in 1997 (*The Man Who Became Sherlock Holmes: The Tortured Mind of Jeremy Brett*), says that Watson saves Sherlock from himself. Without him the detective could have gone mad. "With all his consuming interest in crime he would have lost his mind without someone sensible by his side, someone he could impress, who would listen in awe, who would nag him to eat, remind him to dress properly, warn him of the dangers of cocaine." And even Holmes himself (in 'His Last Bow') says Watson is the one fixed point in a changing world. But he is also a courageous military man and, judging by the gradually increasing size and importance of his Practice as it moves towards more and more impressive addresses, a successful doctor – who also understands psychology. The Holmes-Watson narrative is constantly enlivened by exchanges between the two men, making it more dramatic in form than if there were one narrator. There is an interplay of character which would otherwise be absent. On a more mundane level, a single narrator (unless the reader is willing to suspend disbelief altogether) cannot be everywhere at once. Neither can he be doing everything at once.

For example Sexton Blake, the inspiration of a journalist named Harry Blythe (who first called him Frank and then by a stroke of genius changed the name to Sexton), was largely intended for a juvenile readership and initially appeared in a magazine for boys called *The Halfpenny Marvel*. He had Edward Carter (nickname, Tinker) as a side-kick. But Tinker didn't write up the stories. He was not created to do justice to Sexton by bringing him before a wider public. His job was to run errands, see that the car ticked over efficiently and bring it round from the garage immediately it was wanted. He fetched and carried and was a general factotum. "A sparky street arab" or young vagrant, he lived in the same house as Blake and a rather ill-defined housekeeper. There is no explanation of why this was so, but "the cheery broad shouldered youngster" proved a staunch and efficient ally in many a scrap, or if there was a job to be done. He also kept Sexton's books of press-cuttings carefully indexed and up to date, without which help the detective's efficiency would have been seriously impaired.

As soon as he caught on, Blake moved from North Street, Strand, to an address in Baker Street. Where, according to Jack Adrian in his Introduction to *Sexton Blake Wins!* published by J. M. Dent in 1986, "He looked more like Holmes than Holmes himself due to a less than subtle nose-brows-chin job." And, moving with the times, became an adventurer and a secret agent rather than a detective – being written about by a wide variety of hacks and outlasting his rival by more than forty years. "For while Sherlock pondered, Sexton rolled up his sleeves."

A hero cannot boast of his own successes without becoming a figure of fun, as Conan Doyle shows in his *Adventures of Brigadier Gerard*: "I have told you, my friends, how I triumphed over the English at the fox-hunt when I pursued the animal so fiercely that even the herd of trained dogs was unable to keep up, and alone with my own hand I put him to the sword."

If either Watson or Holmes had been made a figure of fun it would have considerably weakened the impact of the latter's detective prowess. The former couldn't, of course, appear cleverer than the main protagonist if tradition was to be preserved. But neither could the Doctor be entirely without brains. However, this didn't stop Doyle writing (in his book *Memories and Adventures* after discussing Holmes) "I would like to say a word for Watson also, who in the course of seven volumes never shows one gleam of humour or makes a single joke."

Well, he may not have indulged in knockabout farce, but nevertheless a sly gentle kind of fun is there in several passages. One of which leads Holmes to say Watson is developing a certain kind of "pawky humour." Something we suspect when he says that Holmes, when holding forth about one of his cases is, in reality, taking about as much notice of his foil as he would of his own bedstead. Humour implies intelligence, and there are many occasions when Sherlock welcomes his friend's observations.

Holmes is a household name instantly recognised. As Andrew Taylor says in an article written for *The Times* Crime Supplement on October 9th 1999 ('The Books They

Couldn't Kill') "Sir Arthur Conan Doyle dwarfs them all in terms of the influence his creation has had. Since *A Study in Scarlet* was published in 1887, Sherlock Holmes has patrolled the mean streets of London and the equally dangerous homes of country gentry, wielding his superior intellect like a cosh. [He] has spilled into 20th century myth, [thus] becoming a folk hero for the Industrial Age."

In another article for *The Times* Crime Supplement for September 30th 2000 ('A Century of Suspense') comparing Holmes with Inspector Morse, Marcel Berlins says that the two men are remarkably similar. They are "Curmudgeonly classical music-loving bachelors, dedicated to their profession, each with his doggedly faithful and admiring side-kick on whom to unload his brilliant thoughts [and they] clearly form part of the same brotherhood of detection. Even their basic methods – interviews, analysis of clues and insight into human emotions – have remained much the same."

Almost every other character in the canon, from Lestrade to Irene Adler and Mrs Hudson, has been at the centre of one of their own detections – gaining readers solely from their association with Baker Street. Even Moriarty became the central character in books by John Gardner – portrayed, as Mark Campbell says, "as the blackguard he is" – and in a series by Michael Kurland, who turned him into a hero. But it is obvious that (first using the time-honoured names to grab attention) today's authors, playwrights, television programmers and film producers can only get anywhere by making *their* tales more and more bizarre. The charm of the original settings and dialogue, the easy comradeship between two gentlemanly bachelors and the evocation of a by-gone era are not enough.

We have to make Holmes the murderer. Worse than that, perhaps, he does become, intentionally and sometimes unintentionally, a figure of fun. The genre is pushed so far that it's risible, vulgar, or both. Aspects of the canon are exaggerated to the extent that it *is* only the names which are left. As far as I know, however, no-one has devoted almost an entire book to Doctor Watson. But where would Holmes be without this seemingly naive side-kick who, we should not forget, is also his biographer? Beavering away in Baker Street, completely unknown except to a few luminaries at Scotland Yard and some luckless criminals. It's time to redress the balance and let the doggedly faithful (and much put upon) man assume centre stage. In itself this is an unusual place for a foil. But then Watson is unusual. The seemingly social equal of Holmes, but perhaps with a rather awkward, if not dangerous, secret.

Chapter One: On Being Good Old Watson

One evening in 1924 a tall heavily built man, known to the world as Sir Arthur Conan Doyle, sat in his study putting the finishing touches to a book of reminiscences, already referred to in the Introduction, called *Memories and Adventures*. He would not be disturbed. The entire household at 'Windlesham' had strict orders not to come in while he was writing. Neither did the faint rays of the setting sun shining through the windows of the room bother him. After describing how his most famous character, Sherlock Holmes, was based on his old teacher Joe Bell, Doyle went on to say, "He [Holmes] could not tell his own exploits so must have a commonplace comrade as a foil, an educated man of action who could both join in the exploits and narrate them. A drab name for this unostentatious man. Watson would do..."

This was not strictly accurate. Doyle, who said he devoured detective stories of all kinds before trying his own hand at one, also said he decided against the old-fashioned habit of giving characters names which reflected their personalities or their professions. From the evidence of a page torn out of an old notebook, Sherlock began life as Sherringford Holmes. But Watson had the even more outlandish name of Ormond Sacker.

Many years later, the author's son Adrian said his father would never divulge who had been the model for Watson. He himself inclined to a Major Wood, a friend of Doyle senior in his days as a General Practitioner in Southsea and then his Secretary, who had a small office in 'Windlesham', where he sat arranging his employer's numerous lecture tours, and often accompanied the family on their travels abroad. Wood – according to Adrian – was very reliable, intelligent without being brilliant, and a keen sportsman who looked the very picture of a military man. A brief description of Watson in Doyle's story about the blackmailer Charles Augustus Milverton fitted the Major perfectly. "He was a middle-sized, strongly-built man – square jaw, thick neck, moustache..." There was, however, another equally burly man from Conan Doyle's days at Southsea. Dr. James Watson was President of the Portsmouth Literary and Philosophical Society when Doyle was the Secretary and responsible for arranging the weekly talks. Watson's wife carelessly calls him James on one occasion, which lends some support to any claim that the Portsmouth doctor might have to being the model for him. It was certainly more than enough to convince the detective writer John Dickson Carr.

When Doyle was fifteen he came down from Edinburgh to visit his uncle, Richard Doyle. This famous *Punch* cartoonist took him to see the Chamber of Horrors at Madame Tussaud's (which at that time was housed in the Baker Street Bazaar), Henry Irving's performance as Hamlet at The Lyceum, St. Paul's Cathedral, Westminster Abbey and the Tower of London. He also introduced him to John A. Watson who lived next door to Doyle's grandfather in Cambridge Terrace. John A. Watson had served in the First Afghan War, wrote copiously about India and had a fine collection of photographs and souvenirs. Another Watson, first names John Forbes, was an assistant surgeon with the Bombay Army Medical Department. After three years' service in India from 1853-56 he came home and began to promote Indian culture and commerce. This, like John H. Watson and his sleuthing, gradually eroded his medical interests and he became Director of the India Museum in Downing Street. Yet a third John Watson, someone Doyle may have read about much later, met with Major-General Sir Frederick Roberts before they both went up together to Kabul during the Second Afghan War, the conflict in which poor John H. says he was so badly wounded.

But is it necessary to consider only people named Watson, such as Alfred Aloysius who (five years Doyle's senior) attended the same school as he did? In the same way as some writers want Moriarty, a boy also at school with Doyle and a very good mathematician, to be the model for such a villain? The fictional Moriarty is commonly thought to be an amalgam of three people: Alfred Drayson, Adam Worth and James Seward. Major-General Drayson, a friend of Doyle's in Portsmouth, was a mathematician and astronomer, Worth an American crook who stole a painting by Gainsborough, and Seward a notorious nineteenth-century forger. There were also other boys at school with Doyle (both at Stonyhurst and the Jesuit Preparatory School, Hodder), who might be considered as models for his characters. One was Norbert Louis Moran. Was his name altered to that of Moriarty's Chief of Staff, Colonel Sebastian Moran? Did Alfred Aloysius Watson change into Aloysius Doran, father of Hatty Doran in 'The Noble Bachelor'? Some ideas can be pushed too far. When researching a character as we are here, one would hope to find more than just a name. For example, in Robert Louis Stevenson's 'The Adventure of the Hansom Cab' from the book *New Arabian Nights,* Lieutenant Brackenbury Rich comes home from India badly wounded by a sabre cut and weakened by fever in much the same way as Dr. Watson. Bored, lonely and without kith or kin he gravitates to London. Again like Watson. Indeed, much of another tale by Stevenson ('The Dynamiter' in *More New Arabian*

Nights) finds echoes in the Utah section of *A Study in Scarlet.*

Doyle had the opportunity to meet badly injured soldiers from all parts of the Empire soon after he arrived in Southsea. He writes that, in 1882, "A new wave of medical experience came to me about this time for I suddenly found myself a unit in the British Army. The operations in the East had drained the Medical Service and it had therefore been determined that local civilian doctors should be enrolled for temporary duty of some hours a day." Doyle, unlike some of the other doctors in the area, said at his interview that he would do "anything" and was appointed at once by the Principal Medical Officer responsible for Her Majesty's Forces in India. He went on to describe his temporary boss as "A savage- looking medico who proved to be Sir Alexander Home, V.C. – an honour which he had won in the Indian Mutiny. He was in supreme charge and, as he was fierce in speech and in act as in appearance, everyone was terrified of him..."

However, an entry in Home's diary for 13th October 1857, when he was only thirty-one and known simply as a regimental surgeon, rather belies this fierceness. "The wounded are doing very badly – many are dying of lock-jaw – the most horrible death I know. The honours and rewards of the leaders of armies are certainly purchased by incredible suffering by those under them." Three days later he wrote "It is very painful to get such a [mortally wounded] case into Hospital – to know that the man must eventually die and yet be pretending to do him good." It was Home who recommended Private McManus of the Northumberland Fusiliers (the regiment Watson says he joined on his arrival in Afghanistan) for the V.C.

Doyle worked at Netley until shortly before 1885. By

then the situation had eased and all civilian doctors were released from their obligations. But there is no doubt he gained valuable knowledge of military matters, which he was later to use to good effect in his first crime novel. Fourteen years after Doyle's wedding to his first wife, Louise Hawkins, by which time he had given up medicine to become an established writer, he was visited by the American actor William Gillette who wanted his approval of an adaptation of Doyle's play about Holmes and permission to stage it in the U.S.A. Doyle was living with his family at a house which he had built for Louise and called 'Undershaw'. From there he went to meet Gillette at the nearest station, Haslemere. It is said by John Dickson Carr that when the American stepped out of the train Doyle looked at him and saw Sherlock. Gillette, in his turn, looked at Doyle and saw Watson. Was this because Gillette had seen Sidney Paget's drawings for *The Strand Magazine*? Or did he have a picture of the man in his mind from reading the *Adventures*? Drawings of Watson by the artist Sidney Paget were modelled on one of his fellow students at Art School, Alfred Morris Butler. Butler, however, did resemble Doyle; and Paget's studio portrait of Doctor Doyle, though rather stiff, looks a little like him. Somewhat wary about the eyes instead of the genial sparkle one somehow expects from Watson, Doyle massively and self-consciously fills the frame, his thick moustache hiding his mouth. The very picture of a man determined not to give anything away, but secretly afraid that he might.

And was there an element of wishful thinking in Doyle which he transferred to Watson? Speaking of his laziness, the Doctor says he has other vices when he is well. Unfortunately we are not told what these are, apart from womanising, gambling and perhaps dabbling too much in stocks and shares – maybe enough foibles for anyone without adding to them. He asks Holmes to lock up his cheque book, and says that he spends half his wound pension on horses. Doctor Watson, in *The Sign of Four*, has experience of women of many nations and over three continents. He is told by his friend that the fair sex is his department ('The Second Stain') but not Sherlock's because, as Holmes says, women's motives "are too inscrutable" for him. The Doctor is much-married – as well as suspected (in a play called *Angels of Darkness* which was written in 1892 and never published) of philandering with a woman not his wife while practising medicine in the United States.

Doyle said that Joe Bell, his old teacher in the Medical School at Edinburgh University, had sharp piercing eyes, an eagle nose, and striking features – which would seem to fit our conception of the physical appearance of Sherlock Holmes rather well. But Bell also had very dextrous hands, and the habit of studying a patient intently before making what seemed like inspired guesses about his station in life, the tell-tale condition of his clothes and reasons why he had arrived for a consultation. In reality these 'guesses' were the result of his previous scrutiny, coupled with a definite knowledge of disease. Bell said of Doyle, in an interview for *The Pall Mall Gazette* after his pupil became famous, that he had insatiable curiosity and fairly acute senses. He added that the precise and intelligent recognition and appreciation of minor differences was the real and essential factor in all successful medical diagnosis. Carried into ordinary life, and aided by the above traits, "You have Sherlock Holmes, as he astonishes his somewhat dense friend Watson."

But if Bell's comments are applicable to Doyle shouldn't

they also apply to Watson? After all, they are both doctors. And if they don't, doesn't it show Doyle as very ambivalent? While not wishing to put himself forward as the complete Holmes he occasionally oversteps the mark, confusing the reader (and Joe Bell) by making a diagnosis through his Detective. A diagnosis which would more properly belong to Doctor Watson. As such a great admirer of Stevenson, did Doyle create a Jekyll and Hyde figure – one which, unlike the original, had two *separate* bodies but an interrelated intellect? Would he have liked to present himself to the world as an eccentric, mercurial, drug-taking, bohemian? Prey to fits of hard work followed by depression, as indeed was the case in his private life, instead of a staid, reliable pillar of society?

This is, in part, exactly what he does do. Watson says his experience of army life left him with habits rather more bohemian than befits a medical man. He reads *La Vie de Bohéme* and, although he appears to condemn the drug-taking of his friend, and the bullet-pocks on the wall of Mrs. Hudson's establishment put there by that friend, has a huge admiration for Holmes, taking care to record these facts in his writings – along with the jack-knife skewering unanswered letters to the mantelpiece and the tobacco in the Persian slipper. Doyle would like to be Holmes but, ever cautious with his readers and naturally circumspect about his public image, compromises by making us think he is probably more of a Watson. And that Watson, conventional as he may have to be in contrast to his eccentric friend, can only occasionally be a Holmes.

To return briefly to Bell, Doyle wrote in an article for *The Strand Magazine* that his old mentor's powers were "simply marvellous." Gazing quietly at the patient, he would conclude that he suffered from drink by spotting the flask "in the inside breast pocket of your coat." This doesn't seem particularly clever. But he did better with a worn patch on the inside knee of a man's trousers. The placing of this patch was a peculiarity of cobblers because it showed where the patient had rested a lap stone (which is both oily and abrasive) used to smooth leather.

Nevertheless, whatever there is of Doyle in Watson, or whatever there is in Watson from other sources, Helen Constantine says in her Introduction to the 2007 Penguin Classics edition of *Dangerous Liaisons* that "Although most writers of fiction may use models and take from them certain traits of character or situations, real or possible, on the whole, not just for reasons of discretion but more because of the demands of the fiction itself, they are unlikely to commit an exact portrait of any particular person to paper."

We can search for the Doctor as a recognisable physical presence in his many adventures but his complete genesis may for ever elude us.

Chapter Two: On Being an Old Campaigner

John H. Watson, that loyal companion of Sherlock Holmes and chronicler of his investigations, doesn't waste time when introducing himself to the reader. Right at the beginning of *A Study in Scarlet* he tells us that "In the year 1878 I took my degree of Doctor of Medicine of the University of London, and proceeded to Netley to go through the course prescribed for surgeons in the Army. Having completed my studies there, I was duly attached to the Fifth Northumberland Fusiliers as assistant surgeon. The regiment was stationed in India at the time, and before I could join it the second Afghan war had broken out. On landing at Bombay, I learned that my corps had advanced through the passes, and was already deep in the enemy's country. I followed, however, with many other officers who were in the same situation as myself, and succeeded in reaching Candahar [*sic*] in safety, where I found my regiment, and at once entered upon my new duties."

Watson then goes on to say that, although many benefited from the Afghan campaign, it brought nothing but "misfortune and disaster" for him. "I was removed from my brigade and attached to the Berkshires, with whom I served at the fatal battle of Maiwand. There I was struck on the shoulder by a jezail bullet, which shattered the bone and grazed the subclavian artery. I should have fallen into the hands of the murderous Ghazis if it had not been for the devotion and courage shown by Murray, my orderly, who threw me across a pack horse, and succeeded in bringing me safely to the British lines." Ghazis were fanatical Muslims who made a practice of following an Afghan army and, with the enthusiastic help of their wives and daughters, finishing off wounded infidels. Many soldiers besides

Watson had reason to fear their knives, as well as the jezail bullets of the advancing troops. Rudyard Kipling wrote, in 'The Young British Soldier' (from *Barrack-Room Ballads*, 1892), about this rearguard:

> When you're wounded and left on Afghanistan's plains
> And the women come out to cut up your remains
> Jest roll on your rifle and blow out your brains
> An' go to your Gawd like a soldier.

A Northumberland Fusilier, quoted by fellow-soldier, Private H. Cooper, in *What the Fusiliers Did* wrote of the kind of weapon which did for Watson:

> Let us hope o'er the Khyber's rough passes,
> Sweet peace will soon look down and smile,
> And a sound it may stop, which alas! is
> The boom of the nasty jezail.

Regiments in the British Army didn't lose their numbers until sometime after the Battle of Maiwand. This took place in July, 1880, when the 'The Berkshires' consisted of the 49th and 66th Foot. A year later the Cardwell reforms re-arranged regiments according to geographical districts. At the same time the 'linked-battalion system' was established. This allowed for one battalion to be based at home while the other was on active service. When necessary, the battalions on Foreign Service were kept at full strength by drafts of long-serving soldiers sent from the home battalion. At the same time that these reforms were instigated, the infantry became equipped with efficient breech-loading rifles. Edward Cardwell, who was Secretary of State for War 1868-1874, also introduced a system of voluntary short-service enlistment. This was to prove disastrous in the wars with Afghanistan. But he did abolish promotion by purchase. Before that, officers could sell their commissions if they wished to leave the army. This didn't always ensure the best man for the job. For example a good soldier without money found it almost impossible to rise through the ranks.

Early in the Nineteenth Century the need for a secular institution of Higher Education became so great that University College was founded in the Capital in 1827 by radicals who didn't feel the need for any allegiance to the Established Church, or indeed any form of religion at all. Unlike the older universities, it didn't require religious tests for staff or students. As a result it was called "That Godless Institution in Gower Street." A year later, the Anglican Communion founded King's College, also in the Capital; and in 1836 the two Colleges joined together to form the nucleus of the University of London.

During his time there, as well as studying medicine at what we later learn is St. Bartholomew's Hospital, Watson played rugby. In his account of 'The Missing Three-quarter' he shows some grasp of the game (although it seems odd that he is unable to enlighten Holmes as to what 'a right wing three-quarter' might be) and tells us (in 'The Sussex Vampire') the name of the side for which he played – Blackheath. This prestigious Club was responsible for drawing up the Football Association's Rules of the Game in 1863, and later played on a private ground leased to them by a Mr. Robinson.

For Watson to play for a Club of this calibre required not only supreme skill but also very good health. Something which ought to have stood him in good stead in his army career. The names Watson *and* Holmes appear in a list of international rugby players published in *The*

History of Rugby Football Union by O. L. Owen. But unfortunately, for those who would like to think of the two playing the game together as well as the game they *did* play whenever Holmes is said to have remarked that one was afoot, the dates don't fit.

St. Bartholomew's is the oldest teaching hospital in Britain. Founded in 1123 by the King's Jester, Rahere, as a small Priory Hospital staffed by monks with him at their head, it was placed next to a slaughter house outside the City Walls and used primarily for the treatment of lepers. Still on its original site, the medieval buildings have long since disappeared. But the Hospital had been much enlarged over the years by adding research laboratories, as well as the Medical School which Watson attended.

Somewhat surprisingly, the new student never met Holmes during his years of study there. But this may be because, according to the person who introduces him to the man he was later to lodge with, the detective "has never taken out any systematic medical classes." It is also two years since Watson left Bart's. He comes across Holmes in one of the chemistry laboratories. In addition to studying chemistry, Sherlock was also said to spend some of his time in the mortuary beating the cadavers to see how much bruising, if any, could be inflicted after death. But on this occasion he ran towards the ex-soldier and his companion shouting excitedly that he had just discovered a reagent which, because it could only be precipitated by haemoglobin, would be an infallible test for blood stains. Like earlier reagents, it would work if the blood was fresh. But an added advantage was it would also work if the blood stain was of long standing.

Watson cannot see the significance of this. Or why there should be so much fuss over it. Until all is explained to him, that is. Although he doesn't realise it at the time, the long period of his mystification has already begun. Holmes says impatiently that the reagent can be used to catch criminals. Because previous tests were inconclusive, crooks walked the streets years after they should have been hanged. But, in view of the remark Sherlock later made to Watson, there was something else besides a meeting with Holmes which he must have sorely missed among the students during his time at Bart's. This was the presence in the Medical School of "the fair sex." After the pioneering efforts of Elizabeth Blackwell in the Eighteen-Fifties, women were strenuously excluded until 1947.

Regular military medicine began in Britain in 1660 when a Standing Army was raised at The Restoration. It was organised on a regimental basis, and permanent commissions were given to regimental surgeons. A surgeon and an assistant surgeon were attached to each regiment to look after the sick, and to run a small unit hospital. But no medical 'other ranks' were enlisted till after the Crimean War. Before that, medical tasks of a menial kind were covered by using untrained soldiers or by 'press-ganging' local civilians. But, although many surgeons did their duty by their country as best they could without a recognised number of nurses to help them, there were so many scattered companies that the work was made very difficult. Robert Hamilton, a regimental surgeon writing in 1794, was well acquainted with these difficulties. He later also came out strongly against surgeons making matters worse by drinking to excess, gaming and being too interested in sport to attend properly to their patients.

In 1857, the year of the Indian mutiny, a Royal Commission was appointed to inquire into the often very bad sanitary conditions of troops, barracks and hospitals. One of its recommendations was that an Army Hospital Corps should be created as quickly as possible. But the Commission made the mistake of continuing to allow medical care to be in the hands of each regiment. It also failed to insist that commanding officers in the field be responsible for elementary hygiene in their units and so help the medical staff to keep down disease. Cleanliness on parade was no indication of the conditions in which soldiers actually lived. Overworked regimental surgeons without the support of their commanding officers found it difficult to cope.

Come 1860, and after many delays, an Army Medical School was founded at Fort Pitt, Chatham. This shortly moved to the new Military Hospital at Netley, an area near Southampton. The buildings for this great enterprise were placed just above Southampton Water and were thus, in theory, accessible to incoming hospital ships from all parts of the British Empire. In 1865 a pier was built to accommodate them, but it was found to be too short for many. As a result, a new rail link was built from Southampton to the small, sparsely used railway station in Netley village. From there the wounded were transported in carriages, and so jolted about on the rough roads that some patients died before they could reach the wards. By 1899, long after Watson had left the Medical School, another relatively short rail link off this new line went directly to the back door of the Military Hospital and was still there when the United States Army took over the site in 1944. But it would obviously have been better for the wounded if this connection with the Hospital had been made at the same time as the Southampton line was extended to serve Netley village in the 1860's. However, mistakes about how the Hospital should be sited, and its staffing and organisation, caused problems from the start.

Queen Victoria, who would present Victoria Crosses to certain patients after the second Afghan War, wrote in her diary that it was "Really very wrong to send out poor boys like that." She had laid the foundation stone for this vast complex of buildings (which became the principal Military Hospital in Britain) in 1851, coming across the Solent from Osborne House on the Isle of Wight with Prince Albert. But, initially planned to be finished in two years, Netley wasn't officially opened until 1863. A quarter of a mile long, it had 138 wards, a thousand beds, and cost the equivalent of twenty four million pounds in today's money. One block was reserved for sick and wounded officers. Two others were for the rank and file. The ground floors housed consulting rooms and operating theatres. Later another, separate, block would be added. This was for men mentally affected by the nineteenth century's many wars. It would outlast the main buildings which, although demolition began in the nineteen sixties, didn't finally disappear until 1980. The site then became The Royal Victoria Park, with only the Chapel left as a reminder of the old Hospital. As Watson tells us, civilian doctors were trained for service in the army at Netley – where even as a qualified doctor trained at Bart's he would study physiology, surgery and medicine (as well as physical geography, meteorology and even botany and zoology). The Hospital housed the Army Medical Department, the Army Medical School and the Army Hospital Corps already mentioned. Female nurses were eventually recruited to supplement the male orderlies (who had been chosen as much for their strength in restraining patients as for their skill in changing dressings). It was one of these new nurses, Superintendent Mrs. Deeple, who became the first recipient of a Red Cross Medal instituted by the Queen.

The presence of a Medical School meant that Netley

was to be more than a place in which to treat the already sick and wounded and to amputate crushed limbs. It would be in the fore-front of Victorian medical research. But in 1900 it forfeited its cachet, mainly because of the severe losses from disease in South Africa. The School was moved to London, although those who wished to join the Army Medical Service were still trained at Netley. During his course of study Watson specialised in military surgery, pathology and tropical medicine. He also learned what to do when going with a burial party to find and identify officers and men left behind on the battlefield or, in postings like Afghanistan, interred in shallow graves hastily dug by frightened villagers. A study of hygiene was mandatory. The first Professor of Military Hygiene, Surgeon-General Edmund Alexander Parkes, a man with a European reputation, had taught at Netley until he died only two years before Watson's arrival there. This alone meant that the standard of teaching in that subject was still very high, and the Parkes Essay Prize could be won by any would-be army medical officer who took a particular interest in it.

The vast number of casualties brought back to Britain from the Indian sub-continent and other similar theatres of war suffered more from tropical diseases than gunshot or knife wounds, and Sir Almroth Wright (who taught in the Hospital from 1892) worked like a demon to discover a vaccine against typhoid. The military authorities at first refused to use it, throwing case-loads into the Solent from the ships departing for service abroad. These floating boxes eventually got back to a disgruntled Sir Almroth, who departed for St. Mary's Hospital, Paddington, in 1902. Something of a dandy and a ladies' man, he is said to be the model for Shaw's play *The Doctor's Dilemma*. In this drama the Doctor in question has to decide which one of his two patients deserves to live and which one should be allowed to die. Wright, however, disliked the way he was portrayed by Shaw and left the theatre after the first act.

It has been said that Watson couldn't have been a very good doctor if he joined the army. A contemporary article in *The Lancet* even warned newly qualified graduates against doing so. Such an action would harm both a medical man's professional standing and his pocket. But Watson had had no time to prove himself as a practising doctor. He went straight into the army from university, and was so badly wounded at Maiwand he had to be invalided out and couldn't work for some time. However, anyone studying at an institution able to attract men of such calibre as the above (even if Watson didn't make personal contact with them) must have been an asset to the brigades to which he became attached.

To remind him that he was training to be a military man the new recruit wore uniform, took part in parades and field exercises (probably in Aldershot) and learned the principles of service discipline. When not fighting, the greatest enemy to men stationed abroad was boredom. This could be alleviated a little by endless drilling, kit inspections and weapons training. As an officer and an assistant surgeon, Watson could pass the time hunting, gambling and drinking in the Mess. He would also be required to attend a number of formal dinners. Officers also kept pets, mainly dogs, although one is recorded as trying to train a bear, and another was seriously injured by his pet leopard.

It's doubtful if the phlegmatic former rugby player would do anything as exotic as keeping a bear or a leopard. But a pet of any kind could occupy some of his time.

Maybe it was this which gave rise to the suggestion that when he told Sherlock Holmes 'I keep a bull pup' he did mean a real animal. But, all in all, it was an adventurous opening for anyone who could stand the life. Civilian practice depended on patronage, with too many doctors chasing too few patients able to pay for their care. But being in the thick of battle meant medical personnel were as vulnerable as other fighting men and many of them were, like Watson, invalided out of the army.

The 'Fighting Fifth' became known as 'The Northumberland Regiment' in 1782. Their Colonel at that time, who later became the 2nd Duke of Northumberland, was so popular the men paid him the highest compliment they could by asking permission to be known informally by his title. There was also a resolution to enlist only in that county. First formed in 1674 when the Dutch needed help fighting the French, the Fifth recruited sufficient men to form four regiments, one Irish, one Scots and two English. The Commander of the Irish regiment was Lord Clare. Almost immediately he was suspected of disloyalty to the Dutch and replaced by Sir John Fenwick, a Northumbrian.

Sir John was an outspoken and fervent Jacobite. Although never actually fighting against King William III, he was not backward in expressing his admiration and support for the Stuart Cause. Given many chances to change, and not taking advantage of any of them, he was eventually executed 'for high treason' in 1697. He had introduced so many North Country officers to his new command that its national character was changed. It could no longer be called Irish, although for ten years it was stationed in Ireland and used as a police force to curb the activities of a proto-IRA. However, by calling themselves 'The Northumberland Regiment' before all regiments lost their numbers and acquired names the 'Old and Bold', as it was sometimes called, were well in advance of the times. Some years later the Fifth amended its name to 'The Northumberland Fusiliers' from the 'fusil' or match which activated the flintlock muskets they used at that time, before the issue of Lee Enfield rifles. In 1857 the regiment was sent to help suppress the Indian Mutiny, when Victoria Crosses were awarded to Sergeant Grant and Privates McHale and McManus) during the Siege and Relief of Lucknow. Names which are strangely reminiscent of the long gone Irish Brigade led by the obstinate Sir John Fenwick. The Fifth were again in the sub-Continent in 1878, where Watson expected to join them but found they had already gone through the passes which separate Afghanistan from India. Indeed, as we know, he goes so far as to say that he *did* join the Fusiliers; and there has been much speculation and many suggestions why he was transferred so precipitately from that regiment to the Berkshires.

From various hints dropped by Holmes, and certain boasts of his own, the Doctor appears to have been very keen on women. Did he join the army to escape a romantic entanglement, or even some kind of matrimonial trouble? The suggestion that he contacted syphilis seems somewhat bizarre. If an Assistant Surgeon wasn't any use to one brigade because he had some kind of venereal disease how could he be any more use to another? Many of the rank and file, however, did contact the disease in India and there is no reason to suppose officers were entirely exempt from it. But it's much more likely Watson was removed from his brigade because of changes in the way the medical services were being reorganised.

Unification of the medical department had already

begun in England in 1873. But five years later in India it was still working on regimental lines similar to those laid down in the time of Charles II when, as we saw, each regiment was made responsible for its own casualties. However, according to Surgeon-Major G.J.H. Evatt M.D., writing in the RAMC Journal for 1905, such a system would not work in war-time up the Afghan passes, owing to the scattered nature of the troops and the narrowness of the defiles where, according to Rudyard Kipling in the poem 'Arithmetic on the Frontier' from *Departmental Ditties* (1896):

> A scrimmage in a border station-
> A canter down some deep defile-
> Two thousand pounds of education
> Drops to a ten-rupee jezail.

When it became known, as early as September 1878, that an Expeditionary Force under the Command of Major-General Sir Donald Stewart was being organised for combat duty in Afghanistan and would shortly march up to Kandahar, a memorandum on how the medical services should be conducted was submitted to the Government. It had two objectives: to prevent wounded men impeding the fighting progress of healthy troops, and to ensure the best distribution of medical personnel and supplies. Doctors would no longer be commissioned into named regiments. Instead the wounded would be looked after in divisional field and base hospitals. These would be divided into sections for the various corps, and a designated medical officer put in charge of each. Other doctors were to be stationed closer to the combatants, and the wounded grouped together behind the lines. Each regiment would no longer need to indent separately for its own requirements. There would therefore be no duplication of supplies and no waste.

After a great deal of correspondence the 'Précis of Field Medical Services' received Governmental sanction on November 8th 1878. Writing many years later Surgeon-Major Evatt said, "At the very last moment, that is to say, one week before the Army crossed the frontier, a plan of field hospitals as opposed to regimental hospitals was sanctioned, but no one knew anything whatever of the details of the scheme. In three days and practically in the face of the enemy all medical officers and medical subordinates had to be removed from their regiments to the little understood new creations called field hospitals; to hand over every grain of medicines, instruments, and technical equipment, tents, books, documents, and to give and receive receipts on both sides; and finally to draw from the commissariat barrack, ordnance, and transport departments the various equipments needed for the same units the very existence of which was unknown outside the medical department. Few doctors knew what a field hospital was, or how to indent for supplies. As a result, it wasn't until nine o'clock in the evening of the day before the advance to Jamrood that tents for the field hospital were drawn from the Peshawar arsenal." Although Surgeon-Major Evatt was describing what was happening on the North West Frontier this chaotic situation applied everywhere, and led to a great deal of unhappiness among medical personnel who (having lost their regimental rank) were, as he says, "in the indefinite and unsatisfactory condition of being departmental officers attached to a Corps." At the very moment Watson crossed into Afghanistan medical men were being decommissioned and then moved between brigades in the field hospitals.

It was bad luck that the Doctor, in order to accomplish his move, had to travel so far (apparently from Kabul to Kandahar) and under such extremely trying conditions.

Chapter Three: On Being with the Fusiliers

Civilian doctors wishing to join the army went to Netley for five months' training and emerged at the end of their course as assistant surgeons, the equivalent of being made a Lieutenant. But, although a medic enjoyed most of the privileges of an army officer, the decommissioning of regimental doctors (already mentioned by Evatt) meant they had no military rank. Assuming Watson finally graduated from London University in June, 1878 and immediately began five months' training as an army surgeon, this fits in well with the start of his time in Afghanistan. The Second Afghan War began in late November and, when he reached India, the Doctor's regiment was *deep* [my italics] in the enemy's country. Allowing for a sea voyage that at that time lasted for at least four weeks, he wouldn't have caught up with his corps before December.

But could Watson really have met with the Fusiliers by going to Kandahar, even if he does say he found his regiment and at once entered into his new duties? The 'Fighting Fifth' had been in India for twelve years and, when warned for service in Afghanistan on October 18th 1878, expected to be sent up through the Khyber Pass to Kabul. It would have made more sense, if the new recruit was destined for Kandahar, to have been told in Karachi to disembark from the troopship arriving from Britain with other combatants due for service in that area and to join the Berkshires straightaway by going up the Bolan Pass to Quetta and from thence to Charman and across the border into Afghanistan.

One of the Regimental Battle Honours earned by the Northumberland Fusiliers and carried on their Colours is for Afghanistan 1878-1880. But, according to the brochure for the Regimental Museum in Northumberland, the Fifth was not involved in the heaviest fighting there. It was, however, for some years on garrison duty in India, and acted as a reserve corps for men engaged in the Black Mountain Expedition. This was a punitive foray to subdue tribes of Afghan origin living in a Frontier Valley backed by the Black Mountains between Kashmir and Afghanistan. Their depredations had become severe, and a similar expedition twenty years earlier had been too lenient to stop them. When the raids and murders became worse than ever and a party of British troops, in what was then British Territory, were set upon and their officers killed, men of the Fifth (who were stationed at Kuldana in the Murree Hills) were ordered to Kashmir in reprisal. It was at this time that Surgeon Houston rescued a man under heavy fire and, with the help of two privates, carried him to safety. This was, of course, a reversal of Watson's plight at Maiwand. But by that time that gentleman was well into his second Adventure with Holmes and on the brink of being married to Mary Morstan.

In the spring of 1878 the Fifth moved from Allabahad to Chakrata, a healthy Indian hill station. As a result of this move most of them became literally fighting fit. Carrying bayonet, rifle, haversack, greatcoat and seventy rounds of ball ammunition, the rank and file with their mounted officers marched towards the frontier with Afghanistan. At Badshabagh they were told to abandon their white and red uniforms for khaki. One of the men, Private H. Cooper, already mentioned in Chapter Two as the author of the privately printed (1880) *What the Fusiliers Did*, who liked to express himself in poetry wrote of this change:

Being the colour of the ground, it fills our foes with fear
Because they cannot see our men until they are quite
near.

From Saharanapore, a substantial town with a beautiful
botanical garden, the troops went by train to Umballa. They
then travelled past Amritsar to a temporary rest camp at
Mian Mir. These rest camps were normally sited near large
railway stations and taken down during the summer
months. But, in what was called the trooping season, the
men could travel by night, when the temperature was less
enervating, and sleep in the camps by day. Leaving Mian
Mir, the regiment went to Lahore, and then travelled to
Waziristan or 'Little Sheffield' – so called because its main
business was making cutlery. They finally left the train at
Jhelum, the end of the line. After waiting for the baggage,
and transport *dâks* [The word is derived from Hindi, and
applied to relays of horses stationed at intervals along a
route to carry mail and military personnel. A *dâk gharrie*, a
horse-drawn Indian carriage plying for trade. could be hired
by a civilian] the men marched up the Grand Trunk Road to
Rawalpindi, reaching there on the second of November.
They went through the lovely Hassan Abdul Valley, where
they met the band of the Fifty First Regiment of Foot who
played them into camp, and at Lawrencepore halted for
some time to form a brigade.

The Fifth become the Second Brigade of the Second
Division of the Peshawar Valley Field Force, which
remained in reserve guarding the supplies which travelled
up the mountain passes. On the second of December a
forced march of twenty-eight miles to Peshawar was made.
From there the Fifth was sent to garrison Jamrood. Here,

according to H.M. Walker in *A History of The Northumberland Fusiliers 1674-1902* published in 1919 by John Murray, they spent Christmas and "found life very monotonous; all the worry and none of the fun."

To clear the area of raiders and protect convoys, a detachment was sent into the Bazar Valley for a week, when the soldiers were ordered to destroy villages and small forts. This offensive was in the nature of a reconnaissance. A second, more punitive, expedition was sent later. After the Fifth left Jamrood in March 1879, it continued to round up rebellious tribesmen and to burn villages on the way to Lundi Kotal, as well as do convoy duty. But the Khyber Pass had been successfully cleared of hostile Afghans and the supply lines protected.

In June the regiment began its return march to base, resting at Changi near Abbotabad (where the men were accused of bringing cholera to the region) during August. Instructions were received to embark for home the following month. But after the murder in September of Sir Louis Cavagnari, the Envoy sent to negotiate a British presence in Kabul in opposition to the Russian contingent which had been favourably received by the Amir, the Fifth had their sailing orders cancelled. Once again the men were kept in reserve on the North West Frontier, while General Donald Stewart, who had come up from Bombay at the outbreak of hostilities in 1878, was ordered to take a force from Quetta up the Bolan Valley into Afghanistan and re-occupy Kandahar. Major-General Frederick Roberts, who had also been involved in the first campaign of the war, came up again from his base in the Kurram Valley to take Kabul, and to protect the lines of communication.

To conquer Afghanistan, however, would need guns and supplies. A great road was constructed between

Peshawar and Kabul and a chain of forts, barracks and telegraph offices materialised between Jelalabad and the Frontier. These posts needed garrisons, and garrisons depended on convoys. So, as Walker remarks, the Fifth was split up into companies "to hold the forts, guard the road, and bear with cheerfulness the trials of hill warfare with none of the compensations of a good fight."

Two companies garrisoned Khohat from October 1879 until January 1880, while another guarded a convoy as far as Landi Khotal. They were later joined by two more companies and allowed to take part in a short expedition to drive a party of rebels across the Kabul River. In February one hundred men of the Fifth escorted guns from Dakka to Jamrood, meeting some opposition (which they overcame) on the way. In April 1880 the regiment left Landi Khotal for Jelalabad, subduing tribes of hill men, blowing up their forts and burning their villages as they went. This work continued until after the accession of the Amir Abdur Rahman, when the 'Northumberland Regiment' finally left for home. They arrived at the Anglesea & Cambridge Barracks in Portsmouth in December. So that, according to Walker, "They inadvertently turned their backs on the tragedy of Maiwand, and the glories of that final march from Kabul, and the victorious end." Major-General Roberts, however, said of their courage and cheerfulness under hardship that "There is not a better regiment in Her Majesty's service than The Northumberland Fusiliers."

If Watson had been detailed to join the Fifth in India for a relatively quiet life on the Frontier (in spite of the marauding tribes) he would have travelled to Bombay by sea from Karachi, and then gone by rail to Delhi by way of a line coming up from Calcutta at Allahabad. Once in Delhi, he would have boarded the Sind, Punjab & Delhi

Railway to Amritsar, travelling along a 300 mile stretch of rail which had been completed by 1870. This line made it possible to move troops quickly to this strategically sensitive area and so was of immense importance when it came to engaging the enemy.

Evatt says that The Grand Trunk Road, built by the Moguls and leading on from Amritsar to Peshawar, was thronged with lumbering bullock carts and heavily loaded camels. Troops were at all the staging posts, and officers ordered up for special duty found it difficult to join their corps due to the lack of the transport *dâks* already mentioned. At that time what was needed for supplies and reinforcements to reach the Front with any speed and without prohibitive cost to the State was, as Evatt points out, the all important railway line to the Khyber mouth. This, however, was not completed until 1925, when it left the plain of Peshawar at Jamrood, climbed to Lundi Kotal, and from there went over the Pass to the Afghan Frontier.

In December 1878 four companies of the 66th Regiment of Foot ('The Berkshires') sailed from Bombay to Karachi, and in April 1880 marched to Kandahar. Did Watson make the hazardous journey from Kabul to Bombay – the overland distances were (and are) immense – and go from there to Karachi with them? Life would have been a little easier if he'd been commissioned immediately into that regiment after finishing his course at Netley. Sailing out from England on the troopship to Karachi, taking a train from there to Sibi (which has been described as "the hottest spot in all India") and becoming part of a horse and camel 'caravan' across the mountains for the twelve 'stages' of one hundred-mile marches to Quetta, followed by seven stages from Quetta to Chaman and (after crossing the Frontier into Afghanistan) six more one-hundred-mile marches to his final destination, would surely have been enough for any raw recruit without adding to his difficulties by involving him with the Fusiliers. Two companies of the 66th *were* in Kabul and marched with Major-General Frederick Roberts [his rank varies with each report] to the relief of Kandahar in August 1880. But this was more than a month after the battle of Maiwand. Confused as Watson sometimes seems, he couldn't be in two places at once. Did he, perhaps, mistake Kandahar for Kabul when he said "I found my regiment and at once entered upon my new duties"? Was he removed from his brigade to the Berkshires while in Kabul and then removed again to join that section of the regiment destined to fight the huge Force led by the violently anti-British Governor of Harat Province, Ayub Khan? It hardly seems likely, in spite of what is now known about military incompetence at the time.

To add to the confusion, Watson says in 'The Cardboard Box' that he saw service in India as well as in Afghanistan. This service had trained him to stand heat better than cold, and a thermometer at 90 degrees "was no hardship". Did he mean by this that in 1878 he travelled round and round, in full kit under a blazing sun, trying to find out exactly where his corps had got to? Or does it show that he did after all go from Bombay to Karachi, both of which were in India then, and spent over a year doctoring the Berkshires (including his friend Colonel Hayter who was later to prove so hospitable in 'The Reigate Squire') and *not* the Northumberland Fusiliers, until he went up with the regiment to Kandahar in April 1880?

After the disastrous defeat at Maiwand the surviving troops, and the Garrison at Kandahar, were both under siege. This state of affairs lasted until Roberts arrived with his troops from Kabul. Perhaps the Doctor's terrible experiences muddled his mind a little. Once he got back to the British lines he says he was taken to the base hospital in Peshawar. This was a very difficult journey from Kandahar, and presumably he had to wait until after the siege was lifted. So did many other wounded officers and men. Recovering from his injuries and the hardships of the campaign, Watson was suddenly struck down by enteric fever. This could only have made his situation even worse.

Forgetting many years later how devastating this illness had been to him as a very healthy new recruit, Watson says in 'The Stockbroker's Clerk' "The man whom I found myself facing was a well-built, fresh complexioned young fellow with a frank, honest face and a slight, crisp, yellow moustache. He wore a very shiny top hat and a neat suit of sombre black, which made him look what he was - a smart young City man, of the class who have been labelled Cockneys, but who give us our crack Volunteer regiments and turn out more fine athletes and sportsmen than anywhere in these islands."

The masterly 'but' reveals the class-consciousness inherent in Watson's remark, making it less acceptable to modern readers. But, as Watson well knew, it was the young fellows without experience of army life who suffered the most. Eager to join up in the short term, they were unprepared for pitched battles and the privations of war. Lacking the power to withstand fatigue and hardship, the young succumbed to disease, and particularly enteric fever, at twenty times the rate of veterans with over seven years service. This was especially true if the new recruit wasn't in the best of health to begin with and was stationed at a particularly unhealthy cantonment such as Landi Kotal.

In general the more malodorous the area the more chance of disease, including cholera. Broadly speaking, there was a clear line of demarcation between the fevers prevalent at different seasons in the Peshawar and Khyber valleys - where the fevers of the hot season ranged from the slight and ephemeral to the deadly serious, and the dreaded Peshawar fever sometimes caused half companies to go sick and flood the field hospitals.

In autumn and winter there were agues, remittent fevers and dysentery and it was difficult to gauge what effects these last three would have on the long-term health of the sufferer. They sometimes lasted for years, increasing the probability of catching other fevers in the future. Neuralgia, diarrhoea, diseases of the spleen and liver and pigmental changes in the blood and viscera might all be traced back to an illness caught on active service. This perhaps explains Watson's need for rest at the beginning of his association with Holmes. It may also be the reason why he often refers to it, especially in the early part of the canon. It was not easy to avoid drinking tainted water, a prime source of sickness. But, even as late as the Boer War, inoculation against enteric, or typhoid, fever had not been made compulsory. Typhoid made men dizzy and gave them a temperature of over a hundred degrees. It ulcerated the lining of the intestines and precipitated constant bowel movements of the vilest smell. It was the most deadly kind of contagion and, as John Dickson Carr says in his *Life of Sir Arthur Conan Doyle*, "Death from it is not pretty either."

Watson caught enteric fever just as he was getting over the wound received at Maiwand. No wonder he was floored by it, even if, as supposed earlier, he had started off as a robust rugby player and thus in the very best of health. He arrived at the base hospital "worn with pain, and weak from the prolonged hardships which I had undergone." He was so ill his life was "despaired of." It is highly unlikely he could have recovered sufficiently to be sent home on a ship transporting the first troops from Afghanistan if he had really been sent to Peshawar. This is what happened to Surgeon-Major Preston who, according to his Service Record, arrived at Portsmouth Jetty as early as November 1880. Doctor Watson, however, specifically states that he *did* come home on board the *Orontes*. But if it is true that this ship made only one trip to bring home wounded men from Afghanistan as speedily as possible (not an unlikely supposition, given the patriotic panic over Maiwand) then Watson was sent not to Peshawar but to the coastal town of Karachi.

To be on the same ship as some of the other combatants wounded in the Battle of Maiwand would have involved an extremely long journey by transport mule and train from the north-west frontier to Bombay. This would not be at all pleasant for someone "weak and emaciated" who, in addition to his injuries, had been ill for months. From Bombay Watson would have made another long and arduous journey to Karachi by the weekly coastal steamer (the only transport communication at that time) before he could even begin the voyage to Portsmouth. As it is, a severe wound coupled with a long bout of fever which nearly killed him should have prolonged his stay in hospital even beyond that of other sick soldiers: men who missed the *Orontes* but when the Regiment eventually marched out of Kandahar en route for home, to arrive in Portsmouth five months later on the troopship *Malabar*, were still too ill to go with them. Base Hospitals existed not only in Peshawar but also in other parts of the Indian sub-continent. Since military personnel wounded in battles and skirmishes in South Afghanistan were normally sent to Karachi, Watson must, once again, have got into a complete muddle, even though Peshawar was a much more likely place to catch enteric fever than in the relatively healthy coastal town.

As for The Battle of Maiwand, on the first Saturday after the defeat the *Beverley Guardian* [following the London *Times*] reported that 'An appalling disaster has befallen the British forces occupying Afghanistan, similar in character to the slaughter in the Khyber Pass thirty-eight years ago, when our army retired from Kabul, and far greater so far as the loss of life is concerned than the massacre of the British troops at Isandula by the Zulus eighteen months since. There were but few members in the House of Commons on Wednesday afternoon when Lord Hartington [Secretary of State for India] announced in a grave tone that he had serious news to communicate from Afghanistan; and his Lordship read the following telegram [from the Governor-General in Bombay] "Clear the line. Primrose telegraphs today from Kandahar: Terrible disaster; General Burrows' force annihilated. We are going into citadel. Phayre telegraphed to collect what forces we can and march on Kandahar. Posts are being concentrated at Chaman."

The Citadel at Kandahar commanded a view of the City, and the Cantonments (soldiers' quarters, which in India signified a permanent military station) afforded the maximum amount of safety in anything but a safe situation. Lieutenant-General Primrose had, some months earlier, been left in charge of the garrison by Sir Donald Stewart before the latter left for Kabul where, as Commander-in-Chief, he would later give Roberts the men who would march from there to Kandahar to relieve the City. Primrose had telegraphed to Major-General Robert Phayre thinking his men would be the first to reach Kandahar with reinforcements because of their position at Quetta. Significantly, in view of what we later discover about Watson, Phayre's final strength included the Second Battalion the Fifth Regiment of Foot ("The East Yorkshires"). This was ordered up to Quetta from Karachi, where it had been stationed since March, 1880.

In London plans were made to transfer troops immediately from India to Afghanistan, and Lord Hartington promised to send a brigade from Britain. As further details of the disaster were received by Parliament, the Government decided to send more troops. These included some who were stationed in England as part of the relief force under the Territorial System. Phayre kept in close contact with Primrose until the lines of communication at Charman were cut, and gave the first news of survivors to London. He then decided to take his troops up the Bolan Pass en route for Kandahar.

So it was that, on a blazing hot day in August, a column of fully armed military men marched from the railway station at Sibi towards Quetta. The temperature stood at 130 degrees Fahrenheit, and there had been no rain for two years. Each man was in a full fighting kit more suitable for service in Europe; and the heavy khaki jackets and trousers they wore made the intense heat almost unbearable. Red-rimmed eyes looked out from under uncomfortable headgear, and sweat, which would later freeze in sub-zero temperatures, soaked weary bodies and made cut and blistered hands almost too slippery to handle a rifle.

The poetic Private Cooper said of the hardships encountered when marching towards Kabul that, although it was cool up in the hills, as the men went towards the plains the temperature increased dramatically: 'Our clothes were wet with honest sweat, and blistered were our feet. And as we marched along that day we suffered from the heat.' Not brilliant poetry, but it vividly conveys the discomfort of marching through the Indian sub-continent on the way to Afghanistan. It also shows what Watson must have suffered if he had really been trying to join the Fusiliers. The amateur poet soon got tired of trying to write his account in verse and finished the rest of it in prose. He said that on the way from Lawrencepore to Peshawar his regiment made a twelve day stop at Nawshera, which was "One of the hottest places found upon the plain of India." Nothing could be seen there, "except a plain of burning sand, which seemed to be almost red hot..." And men died from heat apoplexy.

There is no reason to suppose that conditions were much better for the brigades going towards Kandahar after the Battle of Maiwand. The defiles were extremely narrow, often forcing the men into single file. The dust in places was six inches thick. Overhanging rocks threatened to fall and crush the column at every step, impeded as it was by the bodies of dead and dying baggage animals as well as camel trains carrying supplies. According to the poetic private turned prose-writer, "A dying camel is a most pathetic sight: the poor beast dies in harness, carrying his load to the death, and then when he cannot bear the burden [any] longer he sits or rather drops down with his legs under him and never moves again until the moment when death comes to his relief, when he falls over to one side, gives a low moan and a few convulsive struggles and is no more."

In addition to their other privations, the men going up

the Bolan Valley were tormented by thirst. But the brackish water they had to drink only made matters worse. Not only did it do little to relieve them but it caused many, especially the most recently drafted, to fall dangerously ill. A scribbled note in a Regimental Diary records the effect of these hardships on the young, saying that the soldiers of the last draft of 294 rank and file could not withstand the privations "owing to their want of physique". This want of physique was probably due, not only to youth and lack of experience, but also to an impoverished upbringing. Joining the army meant danger. But it also ensured adequate clothing and usually ample, if boring, rations. When Roberts returned to England he complained that it was the short service enlistment of young volunteer soldiers without experience which caused so much sickness in the ranks. As a result of this protest, men had to undertake to be with the colours for at least seven years, followed by five years in the reserves.

Chapter Four: On Being in the Criterion Bar

Watson says that when he returned from Afghanistan "I had neither kith nor kin in England." And Holmes remarks in *The Sign of Four*, "Your father, if I remember right, has been dead many years." But the Doctor's watch, which Holmes is examining as a result of a challenge to his deductive powers, has been recently cleaned and so robs the sleuth of his "most suggestive facts." Watson agrees the watch has been cleaned before being sent to him on the death of his brother. But the two men have already been together long enough to solve the problems of *A Study in Scarlet* and 'The Speckled Band'. This suggests that he wasn't entirely without kin on his immediate return from the war. Maybe his brother lived abroad, or in a part of Britain other than England. There is a mention of a visit to Australia. Whatever the situation, Watson gravitated to "that great cesspool" London and took up residence in a hotel in the Strand.

This was rather an expensive place for a young ex-soldier on a sick-leave pension of eleven and sixpence a day to be, even if as a private hotel it was not licensed to sell spirits. Ruminating on whether he should find cheaper lodgings or leave London altogether, Watson wandered into the Criterion Bar, perhaps by way of Trafalgar Square, Pall Mall and either the Haymarket or Regent Street. Although the address of the Criterion was 224 Piccadilly, it is actually in Piccadilly Circus. Be that as it may, the Doctor went inside the building, met Stamford ("who had been a dresser under me at Bart's") and invited him to lunch at the Holborn.

Students studying surgery became dressers in their final year. They were then assigned to a particular house surgeon. Watson's remark implies that Stamford was a senior student and he a houseman working at the Hospital, perhaps while completing his Doctoral Thesis. Quite possibly this was an unpaid part-time post, as Watson would not have been on the staff. Many years later Sherlock Holmes was to demonstrate, in *The Hound of the Baskervilles*, why he thought Doctor Mortimer couldn't be on the staff of Charing Cross Hospital. Only a man with an established London practice could be that. And he wouldn't drift into the country. So Mortimer must have been a house surgeon or house physician. But, in the Detective's opinion, this was little more than a senior student. Having given Watson a small amount of praise in 'Silver Blaze', he wasn't going to allow him to profit too much by it.

Dressers were of even less account than housemen. In a book written by Sir Arthur Conan Doyle called *Round the Red Lamp* a third year student points out the important men in the operating theatre to some first years. "That's Peterson. He's the skin-grafting man, you know. And that's Anthony Browne, who took out a larynx successfully last winter." The question "Who are the two men at the table?" receives an off-hand answer from the more experienced third-year who retorts, "Nobody – dressers. One has charge of the instruments and the other of the puffing Billy. It's Lister's antiseptic spray you know, and Archer's one of the carbolic acid men. Hayes is the leader of the cleanliness-and-cold-water school, and they all hate each other like poison."

Anthony Browne is obviously Patrick Heron Watson. He was an Edinburgh surgeon who, according to the Dictionary of National Biography, "endeared himself to his patients" – perhaps because he was particularly skilled and swift when operating on them and had, like Joseph Bell, a very good bedside manner. In 1861 he published *The Modern Pathology and Treatment of Venereal Disease*, and six years later wrote (in collaboration with a surgeon called Holmes!) a *Manual of the Operations of Surgery*. Even before the introduction of Lister's method of antiseptic surgery Heron Watson had excised hip and knee joints, as well as removing a patient's diseased larynx. As regards his other activities, he was using plaster of Paris to preserve medical specimens long before the criminologist Hans Gross recommended it to preserve footprints. This shows he was well in advance of the scientific discoveries which would later be used to help detection. In *The Sign of Four*, first published in February 1890, Holmes shows Watson a book he has written. This has the cumbersome title *Upon the Tracing of Footsteps, with Some Remarks upon the Uses of Plaster of Paris as a Preserver of Impresses* and reveals that Sherlock too was well in advance of most of the rest of the world. Hans Gross, whose manual on criminology came out a year later, listed and discarded six ways of preserving footprints before deciding in favour of plaster of Paris as "The only good method."

There were at least three schools of thought when it came to avoiding sepsis, the putrefaction of a wound when germs enter into it. But the basis of Lister's method was the use of carbolic acid. He experimented for years to find suitable dressings, and in 1855 went to Edinburgh Infirmary as an Assistant Surgeon. He became a friend of Patrick Heron Watson and succeeded to the Chair of Clinical Surgery in 1869. By 1877 "the apathetic London surgeons" were still not using his methods and he came south to accept the Chair of Surgery at King's College. It is interesting to note that at about the time when John H. Watson was nearing the end of his course of study at Bart's the various controversies surrounding surgery were still going on. Killing germs already in the operating theatre, however, was a great step forward. It gave way eventually to the more effective aseptic procedures, which are designed to prevent them getting there in the first place. Archer, the surgeon everyone is waiting for and who is to perform the procedure of particular interest to the blasé third year man, comes into the operating theatre followed by his houseman, and "a trail of dressers, who grouped themselves into the corners of the room" ready to hand instruments and restrain the patient. However lowly they were thought to be, they would gain valuable experience in surgery and Watson, like Stamford, would have become one sometime during his time as a student before passing his undergraduate degree and having a dresser of his own. For a long time, however, medical men acted upon 'the one thing cures all' principle. A large brown jug containing a mixture of cod liver oil, iron and other noxious substances stood in the front hall of Bart's for years. And out-patients were routinely given a dose or two out of it. Young Stamford, however, although he isn't in awe of Watson, is prepared to give him his due and happy to have lunch with him. But drinking in the Criterion Bar (also known as 'The Long' or 'The American' Bar) if the state of one's finances is "alarming" isn't very wise. We can only suppose depression sent him into that particular hostelry – which was new and bright, having been built in 1873 on the site of The White Bear, one of the busiest coaching inns in central London.

Comparing Britain with Germany, Jerome K. Jerome in *Three Men on the Bummel* said of this Bar: "To the medical student, the eater of dinners at the Temple, to the subaltern on leave, London is a wearisome proceeding. The healthy

Briton takes his pleasures lawlessly, or it is no pleasure to him." But, according to Jerome, England gave such a person little chance to be lawless. Whatever games he got up to, whatever Tom and Jerryish behaviour he indulged in, a young man's evening always ended up with a row at the Criterion Bar, and "You can have no idea how unutterably tired one can become of the walk from Piccadilly Circus to the Vine Street Police Court." Presumably when the shenanigans in, or outside, the Criterion became too much for the outraged citizens.

Dining at the extensive and elaborate Holborn Restaurant in Little Queen Street wasn't cheap. It says much for this forcibly retired army surgeon's degree of loneliness (and his open-handedness) that not only did he enthusiastically welcome someone who "in the old days had never been a particular crony of mine" but was willing to pay for both the lunch and the cab, and certainly spending his money freely As to his sharing lodgings with Holmes, in 1887 the wealthy industrialist Charles Booth began a study into the conditions of life and labour of the four million inhabitants of London, at that time the largest as well as the richest city in the world and covering an area of 117 square miles. He did this at his own expense over a period of seventeen years, and published his results in seventeen volumes. The main purpose of this monumental and influential work was to try to estimate as accurately as possible the number and proportion of families living in misery in the Metropolis. Booth also wanted to find out how many citizens lived in poverty, decent comfort or luxury.

To do this he devised a system of 'classes'. The lowest class contained occasional labourers, loafers and semi-criminals. Then came the 'very poor' who relied on casual earnings. The next two classes contained those workers who had intermittent or small regular earnings. Workers above the poverty line belonged to two more divisions: those earning standard wages and those who were good class labour employed in a good trade. These he labelled the 'comfortable' working class, which included all servants. The two groups with the highest standard of living, those who employed servants, Booth labelled 'Middle' and 'Upper': thus perpetuating the idea of a Class System for years to come.

We can deduce from this that Doctor Watson belonged at least to the middle classes through his attendance at public school, his medical training and his army-officer status. Moving out of the hotel into Mrs. Hudson's establishment does, however, present a slight problem. Having a large airy sitting room and two bedrooms meant that he and Holmes were not, like some of those in Booth's other classes, confined to one room. But Mrs. Hudson, although their landlady, showed in Holmes' clients (at least until Billy the pageboy arrived on the scene) and provided the food, even if she perhaps didn't prepare it. Was she part of the 'comfortable' working class of Booth's system of classification? She had a little maidservant of her own (*A Study in Scarlet*) And was the house her's, or were Holmes and Watson helping to pay her rent? What happened to her many years later, and how did her status change, when Watson went back to his 'old service' and Holmes retired to Sussex to keep bees?

When Watson married he had, with his wife, the use of a whole house – even if part of it served as a consulting room. The couple vary between having one servant and 'servants' – who lock up after the household has gone to bed. It's a servant who calls a cab when the Doctor takes

Vincent Hatherley to consult Holmes in 'The Engineer's Thumb'. Hatherley, although he says he is "an orphan and a bachelor, residing alone in lodgings in London", is a member of at least the middle-classes because of his status as an hydraulic engineer. This is so even though he has earned very little money since qualifying.

"How do I know that you have been getting yourself very wet lately, and that you have a most clumsy and careless servant girl?" asks Holmes in the first investigation which appeared in *The Strand Magazine*. To which the Doctor (who has been puzzling over Sherlock's first observation) replies, "As to Mary Jane, she is incorrigible, and my wife has given her notice." Holmes then explains the reasoning behind both his observations. "My eye tells me that on the inside of your left shoe, just where the firelight strikes it, the leather is scored by six almost parallel cuts. Obviously they have been caused by someone who has very carelessly scraped round the edges of the sole in order to remove crusted mud from it." Watson, or rather his shoe, has been the victim of a "particularly malignant boot-slitting specimen of the London slavey." Careless as her slavey was, however, it's to be hoped that Mrs. Watson changed her mind and decided to give the girl another chance. The very word 'slavey' suggests a little maid-of-all-work. In other words, not someone who could be trained up to become a higher class of servant. And a servant unable to perform even menial tasks satisfactorily, an inefficient slavey summarily dismissed, could not hope to remain (if indeed she ever was) a 'comfortable' member of the working class. She would most likely sink into the lowest form of prostitution.

As far as that goes, Irene Adler was at the other end of the scale. Former mistress of the King of Bohemia and an actress good enough to deceive Holmes, she has her own house in Serpentine Mews. Her former lover calls her "the well-known adventuress." But one of the many paragraphs in Holmes' exhaustive indexes describes her as an opera singer: a contralto talented enough to have sung at *La Scala*. Her letter to Holmes after he has tricked her into revealing the hiding place of a photograph incriminating the King, if correctly transcribed by Watson, reveals that she was trained as an actress and often walks about the streets in male dress, appreciating the freedom it gives her.

Any one of these things would be enough to make her status equivocal in the eyes of respectable Victorians since, according to Kellow Chesney in his account of *The Victorian Underworld*, the connection between prostitution and the theatre was not just a matter of both being centred in the same area of London. Despite the status achieved by some theatrical families, and the care some actresses had always taken of their reputations, prostitutes and women on the stage were still not in wholly separate categories. But Irene's marriage to a lawyer, even if the couple plan to live abroad to escape any possible censure, would probably propel her into Booth's middle class.

Sleeping rough and with no settled home, endlessly roaming the London streets in cut-down trousers and caps too big for them, certain youngsters eked out a perilous existence and were still very much in evidence as late as 1893. This was in spite of Forster's Education Act and Booth's Herculean studies. A kindly Watson speaks genially about them in *The Sign of Four*: "There came a swift pattering of naked feet upon the stairs, a clattering of high voices, and in rushed a dozen dirty and ragged little street arabs." The leader of this bunch of boys is taller and older than the others; and he "stood forward with an air of lounging superiority which was very funny in such a disreputable little scarecrow."

Holmes is less amused. He needs results, and is not going to write up a sanitised account of this particular investigation for city clerks to read. "I want you to find the whereabouts of a steam launch called the *Aurora*, owner Mordecai Smith, black with two red streaks, funnel black with a white band. She is down the river somewhere." The scarecrows are to have a shilling a day each, "and a guinea to the boy who finds the boat." Later Holmes says to Watson, "If the launch is above water they will find her." Of course they will. A shilling a day was riches to them, and a guinea unimaginable.

Having placed Watson firmly in one of the more affluent classes, what of the policemen he met in company with Holmes? According to June Thomson in *The Secret Journals of Sherlock Holmes,* a Detective-Inspector of the first rank earned between two hundred and fifty and two hundred and eighty pounds per annum at the turn of the century, while a second ranker earned seventy pounds per annum less. A uniformed inspector had to be content with fifty-six shillings a week. It's not unreasonable to suppose that in 1887 these figures were somewhat lower. In 1855, at the time of the first Great Train Robbery, the Station Sergeant Dalby had a weekly wage of fifteen shillings. This was the same as that earned by the guard with a sickly child who allowed himself to be bribed by Edward Pierce and was the only member of the gang to go to prison. And things were not much improved thirty years later. The police constable on the beat during the 1880s was a very poorly paid person, earning less than twenty-four shillings for a seven-day week. He could, however, look forward to a pension when he retired. This put the lowest member of the force into the so-called 'comfortable' working class (although he was still very vulnerable) and the highest paid in Booth's middle class.

In *A Study in Scarlet* Holmes and Watson visit John Rance in Audley Court, which Watson tells us "was not an attractive locality." Rance has "a small brass slip" on the door of his "sordid" house, but the pair have to circumnavigate "dirty children" and "discoloured washing" to get to it. When speaking to him of Lestrade and Gregson, Holmes uses the prefix 'Mr.': 'Mr. Lestrade', 'Mr. Gregson', just as they do when speaking to him. Firm indications of the differences in social class. The newly awakened and still sleepy constable (he has been on night duty for eight hours) reveals that he failed to spot the murderer. A frustrated and angry Holmes retorts that he will never rise in the force. "That head of yours should be for use as well as ornament. You might have gained your sergeant's stripes last night." But poor Rance is no sharp-witted street arab. He is also rather nervous as well as unobservant, and may lose his pension, house, brass slip, etc. and sink lower down the social scale if he doesn't buck up. His surliness before his 'betters', and a tendency to blame circumstance rather than himself, won't help either.

Colonel Hayter of 'The Reigate Squire' and the Honourable Ronald Adair ('The Bruce-Partington Plans') are definitely at the top of the social scale. As is the Reigate Squire himself and Dr. Roylott of 'The Speckled Band', in spite of their murderous intentions. Colonel Sebastian Moran is also decidedly upper class. In answer to Watson's astonished comment in the investigation known as 'The Empty House', "The man's career is that of an honourable soldier", Sherlock says of him: "Up to a certain point he did well. He was always a man of iron nerve, and the story is still told in India how he crawled down a drain [perhaps Watson's army officer slang for a *nullah* or water course when he came to write up the investigation] after a wounded man-eating tiger. There are some trees, Watson, which grow to a certain height and then suddenly develop some unsightly eccentricity. You will see it often in humans."

Holmes' theory is a genetic one. Somewhere in the Colonel's pedigree is an influence that has caused him to go to the bad. He became the "epitome of the history of his own family." This is in spite of being the offspring of Sir Augustus Moran, C.B., once British Minister to Persia. Earlier Holmes says to Moran, "I wonder that my very simple stratagem could deceive so old a *shikari* [hunter or hunter's attendant]. It must be very familiar to you. Have you not tethered a young kid under a tree, lain above it with your rifle, and waited for the bait to bring up your tiger? This empty house is my tree and you are my tiger."

The following true account of a tiger hunt appeared in *The Strand Magazine* for December, 1897 reads: 'Mr. C. Allan Cooke, after a three night vigil in a tree, heard the barking and screeching of monkeys which showed a tiger was present. It did not, however, stop to drink and Mr. Cooke was able to take a shot at it and wound the animal, "which immediately bounded off without a sound; he passed right under my tree and up the side *nullah* to my left." Getting down from the tree with his attendants, Mr. Cooke followed a trail of blood spots for a quarter of a mile "and then returned to collect all the shikarees before going any further." The end of it was that the tiger was discovered in a deep cave, wounded and furious with pain. The entrance to the cave was long and narrow – a sort of parallel passage which could be entered only by sliding at full length. Mr. Cooke's attendants feared to enter, with an angry animal at the other end to meet them, but the hunter himself, at the peril of his life, fearlessly undertook the job, and with one shot put an end to the beast.'

Did Doctor Watson read this and use it later? His very slightly changed account of a tiger hunt (the cave has become a drain) published in 1903 allowed him to do what Holmes pretended to abhor: sensationalise their investigations together. It was obviously a temptation an old soldier, who had once served in India and Afghanistan however briefly, couldn't resist.

At the moment, however, we must leave Doctor Watson with Stamford who, although nothing more is heard of him, is the important figure who introduces the two men to each other – thus becoming, as Professor S. C. Roberts remarks in *Holmes and Watson – A Miscellany* published by the OUP in 1953, "One of the great go-betweens of history, a liaison officer of Literature."

Chapter Five: On Being in Afghanistan

Holmes (as we learn Watson will always let him) astounds his new acquaintance as soon as the two men meet in the chemistry laboratory at Bart's. Immediately after being introduced to one another by Stamford – 'Doctor Watson, Mr. Sherlock Holmes' – the latter remarks, "You have been in Afghanistan, I perceive." This sets the pattern for their future partnership: he will seem eternally omniscient, Watson seem eternally puzzled.

Later, explaining how he had come to deduce where Watson had been pursuing his aborted army career, Holmes says, "From long habit the train of thoughts ran so swiftly through my mind that I arrived at the conclusion without being conscious of intermediate steps. There were such steps, however. The train of reasoning ran: 'Here is a gentleman of a medical type, but with the air of a military man. Clearly an army doctor, then. He has just come from the tropics for his face is dark, and that is not the natural colour of his skin, for his wrists are fair. He has undergone hardship and sickness, as his haggard face says clearly. His left arm has been injured. He holds it in a stiff and unnatural manner. Where in the tropics could an English army doctor have seen much hardship and got his arm wounded? Clearly in Afghanistan.' The whole train of thought did not occupy a second. I then remarked that you came from Afghanistan, and you were astonished."

Watson then highlights what was to be another permanent aspect of his relationship with Holmes by remarking, "It is simple enough as you explain it." This in turn gives his fellow-lodger the chance to say, "You know a conjurer gets no credit once he has explained his trick; and if I show you too much of my method of working, you will come to the conclusion that I am a very ordinary individual after all."

This complaint finds an echo in 'The Red-Headed League' when Jabez Wilson laughs heartily and says, "I thought at first you had done something clever, but I see there was nothing in it after all." Holmes says resignedly, "I begin to think, Watson that I make a mistake in explaining and my poor little reputation, such as it is, will suffer shipwreck if I am so candid."

At his first encounter with Watson, however, Holmes' omniscience is at fault. Afghanistan isn't in the tropics. His train of reasoning could have led equally well to South Africa, where Watson could have been wounded just as easily and perhaps become even more tanned. An additional point is that, from the evidence of a page torn out of one of Conan Doyle's notebooks, he was originally meant to be stationed in the Sudan; which again isn't in the tropics. But the massacre of General Gordon, who had been sent out from England to rescue weak and ineffective Egyptian military forces unable to control the country they had occupied, was still very much in the public mind when Watson was on the brink of his literary career. Gordon was a towering figure to the Victorians, although there were some dissenting voices. For example that of Winifred Seebohm, quoted in *A Suppressed Cry* by Victoria Glendinning, who wrote, "I am not a worshipper of Gordon. I am surprised to find from talking to our working men who have relations in the Army that Gordon is not liked by the soldiers under him – they say he was careless of bloodshed. We never did admire him as a whole – he was too mad – and that kind of presumptuous religion makes me shiver. His work amongst the poor and his endurance of hardship were very grand: but many are doing more at the first, and for the latter, it was no more than one expects of every Englishman."

Martin Fido, in *The World of Sherlock Holmes* published in 1998 said, "The alcoholic, homosexual, imperialist and evangelical Gordon was a hero to Watson, who owned pictures of him and the almost equally scandal-tainted evangelical American anti-slavery preacher Henry Ward Beecher." Who was said to be having an affair with Mrs. Theodore Tilton, the wife of a close friend.

But while Ward Beecher largely escaped odium, at least in Britain, the Prime Minister William Ewart Gladstone went from being the GOM (Grand Old Man) of politics to the MOG (Murderer of Gordon) in the public mind. It was obvious that Gordon's death might make it difficult for an ex-army surgeon to get himself published if his adventures had taken place in the Sudan, although there is a sense in which he might also have benefited from the connection. As it is, Watson says in an investigation into the Reigate Squire that he has refrained from publishing an account of the Netherlands-Sumatra Company and the schemes of Baron Maupertuis because these happenings "are too recent in the minds of the public, and are too intimately concerned with politics and finance, to be fitting subjects for this series of sketches." Although the British defeat at Maiwand was a sensation at the time, it faded from the public mind relatively fast. Trying to get into print with an account involving a country where a popular hero and a British garrison had just been gunned down could be definitely dysfunctional. It would only lacerate still further emotions already at fever pitch.

Be that as it may, there was some difficulty in placing Watson's first published work, *A Study in Scarlet*. James Payn, the editor of *The Cornhill Magazine*, liked it – but said it was both too long and too short. There was too much for a story covering one issue, and not enough for a serial. A second publisher kept the tale for two months and then returned it without bothering to take it out of its cardboard cylinder. Ward Lock finally accepted the novella in October 1886 but delayed publication until 1887, when it appeared in a *Christmas Annual.* A year later it was brought out in book form. But although it was noticed favourably by a few reviewers (*The Bristol Mercury* wrote that 'The story is very exciting and well-told') it wasn't until the appearance of 'A Scandal in Bohemia' that the Doctor's narratives really took off.

However, to return to Watson's meeting with Stamford. After pumping his former dresser as much as he dared, Watson decides that it might be a good idea to share lodgings with Holmes. He looks upon it as a happy coincidence that two young men are currently looking for a way to cut down expenses. Holmes, too, is cautious. After the question of strong tobacco has been settled satisfactorily, he asks if there is any other reason why they shouldn't share rooms together. Watson replies rather cryptically that he keeps 'a bull pup.'

This has been taken literally by some writers, who speculate on what might have happened to the dog since it isn't mentioned again. But Watson frequented the Criterion Bar. Did this subtly strengthen the idea that the Doctor was a betting man? In 'Shoscombe Old Place' he pays for his knowledge of the turf with about half his wound pension. An exaggeration, perhaps. But it points to at least some experiences at the race course.

Many outwardly respectable Victorian gentlemen kept dogs specially trained to take part in secret ratting contests. Dogs which were quartered not in the house as pets but in specially constructed cages, often at the end of the garden. It could have been awkward to keep such a dog in rooms which were already cluttered up with chemical apparatus, newspaper files and other paraphernalia essential to Holmes' work as a detective: even if Watson described the lodgings as large, airy and cheerfully furnished. Jack Tracy says in the *The Encyclopaedia Sherlockiana* published by N.E.L.in 1977 that 'to keep a bull pup' is Anglo-Indian slang for having a quick temper. Watson, of course, could easily have picked up this expression during his time as an army surgeon. But, although he is annoyed by Holmes' criticism of his writings and irritated by the Detective's egoism in *The Sign of Four*, the poor man is careful to say, "I made no remark, however." Considering Holmes' bursts of irritation and the way he so often rounds on his phlegmatic friend, the old soldier would appear to be doing himself an injustice in claiming his temper was on a short trigger. It's Sherlock who keeps the bull pup.

But during this first conversation together Watson says he objects to rows because his nerves are shaken. Holmes takes 'rows' to mean discordant noise, and mentions his own violin playing. If Watson meant that he couldn't stand disagreements this implies that he did find it difficult to hold himself in check. It reinforces the idea that 'I keep a bull pup' showed his temper *was* on a short trigger. A real dog could easily be sold or even put down. It would certainly have been difficult to keep it in a hotel. And where might the impoverished Watson find the money for its outside kennelling? There was, however, a revolver called the Bulldog, made originally by Webley and Scott in 1878, and Watson's 'bull pup' just might have referred to a small handgun. However, the American Mail Order Company Montgomery Ward, which began trading in 1872, has in its 1895 Catalogue 'A double action, self-cocking revolver called the Bull Dog'. This was their cheapest gun, costing less than two dollars, and was described as 'not a toy but a good big weapon'. But if Watson was used to calling his old service revolver 'a bull dog' or 'a bull pup' then a gun would prove useful rather than otherwise once he discovered the occupation of his new acquaintance.

Many ex-servicemen kept their old weapons as souvenirs, ones which took up very little room. And having a bad temper, or even a live dog, sounds rather a lame excuse for not sharing lodgings, especially if money is tight. Perhaps Watson in his debilitated state lacked confidence and felt he might become a burden. In which case such talk sounds like some sort of get-out. Is he suddenly afraid that sharing rooms with a stranger might not be such a good idea after all? At the beginning of his literary career, however, Watson seems obsessed by 'bulls', whether dogs, guns, tempers or ornaments. For example the Mormon Enoch J. Drebber of Cleveland, one of the two men murdered in *A Study in Scarlet,* wore a gold pin topped by a bull-dog's head with rubies for eyes.

When he first began to share rooms with Holmes, Watson was so devoured with curiosity to know how his companion passed his time that it came as a great relief to him to be able to head one of his chapters on the Drebber case 'The Science of Deduction.' At last he has discovered what Sherlock does for a living. Indeed, his delight was so great at being taken into his companion's confidence that he uses the same heading for a chapter in *The Sign of Four.* Watson is still recovering from his experiences in Afghanistan, but in spite of that Holmes turns out to be as anxious as ever to show how clever he is. Just as clever as he was, or thought he was, in *A Study in Scarlet.*

The captive invalid who has, however, summoned up enough energy to criticise Holmes for his drug habit, is treated *gratis* to a high flown exposition of the abilities which rightly belong to a unique detective such as Sherlock. He *knows* Watson has been to the Wigmore Street Post Office that morning to despatch a telegram. The Doctor protests that this was done on the spur of the moment. He hadn't let on about it to anybody. But, to Holmes, "It is simplicity itself...so absurdly simple that an explanation is superfluous; and yet it may serve to define the limits of observation and of deduction. Observation tells me you have a little reddish mould adhering to your instep. Just opposite Wigmore Street office they have taken up the pavement and thrown up some earth, which lies in such a way that it is difficult to avoid treading in it in entering. The earth is of the peculiar reddish tint which is found, as far as I know, nowhere else in the neighbourhood. So much is observation. The rest is deduction."

But, says the sorely tried Watson, how does his clever friend deduce the telegram? Once again Holmes delivers the goods. He has been sitting opposite his fellow lodger all morning so is fully aware that he hasn't written a letter. The open desk shows he has plenty of stamps, as well as a bundle of postcards. Why else then would a man go to a post office if it wasn't to send a telegram? This satisfies Watson, although the reader could no doubt think of other reasons for going into a post office, not all of them innocent. But the piece about the reddish clay has been taken directly from Joe Bell who, addressing a particular patient as 'Pat' – "For it was impossible not to see he was an Irishman" – went on to ask the man if he had enjoyed his walk across the Links as he came from the south side of the town. The patient replied that he did, adding ingenuously

"Did your honour see me?" "Well," went on Bell, very much in the manner of Holmes, "On a showery day, such as that had been, the reddish clay at bare parts of the Links adheres to the boot, and a tiny part is bound to remain. There is no such anywhere else round the town for miles." Is this piece of plagiarism the reason some commentators say Watson may have studied at Edinburgh, as well as London, University? When the poor man, having meekly accepted the explanation for the telegram, then asks permission to set Sherlock a more severe test in detection (the one involving the watch) he is bested again by a devastating exposure of his family failings; and is very upset at what he sees as his housemate's perfidy. That is until his mentor explains it all away, giving a virtuoso performance as the Great Detective.

Holmes, however, is merely following the classical pattern of the superior investigator with a supposedly slow-witted foil. As Agatha Christie says in *Death in the Clouds* first published in 1935, "Interesting, by the way, how the technique of the idiot friend has hung on." In an earlier work called *Partners in Crime* she writes, "Once the idiot friend, always the idiot friend. There's etiquette in these matters." Indeed there was, as Olga Katzin-Millar remarks: "Mysteries were solved with a nonchalance more than sublime, millions of Watsons, supremely dim-witted, having a terrible time." Holmes' quotation in *A Study in Scarlet*, from the seventeenth-century French poet and critic Nicolas Boilau-Despréaux, is unfortunate in this context: "An idiot always finds a bigger idiot to admire him." But in this case he wasn't referring to himself and Watson but to the police officers Lestrade and Gregson.

Not everything written so far, however, can be applied to the Holmes-Watson partnership. True, this is uneven.

But although Jack Adrian, already mentioned as the editor of *Sexton Blake Wins!*, calls the Doctor "a dull-witted plodder" and asks, "Where's the fun in ending up feeling like that blockhead Watson every time?" the poor man hardly qualifies as a stupid fool. Holmes is presented in his narratives as "the wisest man I have ever known." But Watson isn't above giving his friend's ego a knock or two when it suits him, as the following exchange from *The Valley of Fear* shows:

> "You have heard me speak of Professor Moriarty?"
> "The famous scientific criminal, as famous among crooks as..."
> "My blushes, Watson!" murmured Holmes in a deprecating voice.
> "I was about to say, as he is unknown to the public."

On another occasion Watson reprimands Holmes (who is refusing to let him come on what might be a dangerous mission) quite sharply, saying: "My resolution is taken. Other people beside you have self-respect and even reputations." However, what Watson has to do is provide a framework where Holmes can show his genius. His natural modesty and gift for self-effacement, coupled with a clear, readable literary style, enables him to do this admirably. And, although Sherlock complains about the 'romantic' tinge of his tales, this touch humanises a man who might otherwise be seen simply as a cold and calculating machine – a brain on legs.

Holmes is presented as top dog, most of the time, and makes rings round the official police in the shape of Lestrade, Gregson and other luminaries. He is also eccentric. For example Watson doesn't gloss over the tobacco in the Persian slipper and the indoor pistol practice. Holmes can, as well, be condescending to everyone when the time comes for explanations. But he is presented essentially as a gentleman and so must behave modestly occasionally, if only to highlight his extreme capabilities. However, Watson's accounts of their Adventures together stay within a well-tried mould. The pointing finger of unjust suspicion occurs in at least three of the investigations: 'The Five Orange Pips', 'The Bruce-Partington Plans' and 'The Priory School'. Suspicion also falls, very heavily and unjustly, on Watson's old school friend Percy Phelps in 'The Naval Treaty'. In 'The Norwood Builder', as well as the solicitor McFarlane coming under undeserved suspicion, there is a variation on the locked room convention. There is also a staged ruse to reveal the culprit, together with examples of the unimaginative police officer and of the psychological approach.

Watson, himself a believer in the psychological tenet of the *idée fixe,* reports Holmes as saying to a Scotland Yard man, "You do not add imagination to your other great qualities; but if you could for one moment put yourself in the place of this young man, would you choose the very night after the will had been made to commit your crime? Would it not seem dangerous to you to make so close a relation between the two incidents? Again, would you choose an occasion when you are known to be in the house, when a servant has let you in? And, finally, would you take the great pains to conceal the body and yet leave your own stick as a sign that you were the criminal? Confess, Lestrade, that all this is very unlikely."

In 'The Retired Colourman' he remarks to McKinnon, apropos himself, "You get results, Inspector, by always

71

putting yourself in the other fellow's place, and thinking what you would do yourself. It takes some imagination, but it pays." The police also blunder badly when they arrest Fitzroy Simpson for the murder of the trainer Straker, who has been killed by a horse in 'Silver Blaze'. Watson is also happy to use 'The Solution by Surprise' in his accounts. This is in spite of Bell's view to the contrary, expressed in several publications after the Doctor and his friend Holmes had become household names, that there is no trickery in any of the stories. Sherlock says to the policeman in *The Valley of Fear*, "We sometimes set the scene to glorify our results. The blunt accusation, the brutal tap on the shoulder – what can one make of such a denouement? But the quick inference, the subtle trap, the clever forecast of coming events, the triumphant vindication of bold theories – are these not the pride and the justification of our life's work?" He says to Watson, "It is not really difficult to construct a series of inferences, each dependent on its predecessor and each simple in itself. If, after doing so, one simply knocks out all the central inferences and presents one's audience with the starting point and the conclusion, one may produce a startling, though possibly a meretricious, effect."

All of which comes perilously close to Joe Bell's condemnation of what he called, in an article ('Mr. Sherlock Holmes') for *The Bookman*, 'shilling shockers' as distinct from his high opinion of Holmes' way of working. In shilling shockers "crimes were solved not by logic but by Extraordinary Coincidences [and] preternaturally gifted detectives, who make discoveries by flashes of insight which no one can understand..."

It would seem, however, that Holmes felt Watson never recognised this meretricious behaviour and continued to be amazed during their entire association. In 'The Blanched

Soldier', Sherlock (somewhat unfairly considering the number of times he drags Watson away from wife and home) says, "Speaking of my old friend and biographer I would take this opportunity to remark that if I burden myself with a companion in my various little inquiries it is not done out of sentiment or caprice, but it is that Watson has some remarkable characteristics of his own, to which in his modesty he has given small attention amid his exaggerated estimates of my own performances. A confederate who sees your conclusions and course of action is always dangerous, but one to which each development comes as a perpetual surprise, and to whom the future is always a closed book, is, indeed, an ideal helpmate." This devastating critique, of course, tells us that in his opinion Watson has much to be modest about.

Chapter Six: On Being able to deal with Powder Blackening

Immediately before his virtuoso performance in *The Sign of Four* on the red clay sticking to Watson's shoe leather, and a little later the cruel exposition of his brother's weaknesses, Holmes says that detection should not be tinged with romance (another hit at poor Watson). It should be an exact science. It would not be surprising, therefore, to hear of him using every available method of Medical Jurisprudence, as Forensic Science was called in his day, to solve crimes. For example, the Doctor tells us in 'The Naval Treaty' that, during a train journey to Woking, "His [Holmes'] conversation, I remember, was about the Bertillon system of measurements, and he expressed his enthusiastic admiration of the French savant."

By the time this story is supposed to have taken place most western countries had regular police forces and the so-called Bertillon System, introduced into France in 1883 by the criminologist Alphonse Bertillon (1853-1914) Head of the Identification Department of the Prefecture of Police in Paris, was based on the phenomenon that no two people have the same combination of body measurements; and that certain measurements, e.g the length and breadth of the head, the size of the left foot and the size of the left forearm (all of which Bertillon measured using callipers) stay more or less constant from adolescence to old age. Using photographs taken from every angle, and systematic descriptions of the physical characteristics of his subjects, along with these measurements, Bertillon compiled a huge dossier of suspects.

In spite of Sherlock's admiration, however, the method was unfortunately somewhat limited. It was only potentially successful if there were witnesses to a crime or, more usefully, if a habitual criminal with a record was posing as a first offender under an assumed name. But, using the method alone, it was very difficult to link a particular person to a particular crime without other evidence. The method also had the added disadvantage of not being easily searchable.

Even so, *Bertillonage* swept the world, with an Anthropometric Registry being established in Britain in 1883. It would not be altogether abandoned until some weeks after Bertillon's death and the final acceptance of fingerprinting. This had been used in China for centuries to discover who were the true owners of certain important documents –and in Kipling's *Kim* the Indian merchant, Mahub Ali, is able to use his thumb print as his signature because it has a distinctive scar. The phenomenon of fingerprints being different for each individual had been recognised as early as 1820 but a means of classifying them wasn't developed; and in 1858, when an Examining Magistrate in India named William Herschel used them to detect monetary fraud and sent an enthusiastic letter to the Inspector-General of Police in Bengal on the subject, his communication was dismissed as "The fevered wanderings of a man weakened by dysentery."

In spite of the British polymath Francis Galton's pioneering work in the middle eighteen-sixties on the differences between whorls, arches and loops in fingers and thumbs, as well as some of the discoveries coming out of a Belgian university at about the same time, the science of fingerprinting didn't gain much credence in Europe until considerably later in the nineteenth century and was not used routinely in Britain until 1902, when Edward Richard Henry (formerly an Inspector General of Police in Nepal and afterwards an Assistant Commissioner at Scotland

Yard) founded the Central Fingerprint Branch. He had recognised a way of classifying fingerprints in 1896, and took up his post at 'The Yard' in 1901. Just in time for Holmes to know about them and be able to deride a thumb print found by Lestrade on an inside wall of a house belonging to the villainous Jonas Oldacre. And for Watson to tell us what really lay behind the manufacturing of it by the Norwood builder.

An excited Lestrade draws attention to a bloodstain and says to Holmes, "You are aware no two thumb marks are alike?" Sherlock replies that he has heard something of the kind. He is then invited to compare the stain with a wax impression of the suspect's right thumb taken by Lestrade's orders that morning. The suspect, however, is in gaol, and Holmes *knows* the print was not there the day before. To Watson's relief, there's hope for the young man yet. He reveals that the intended victim was tricked into leaving his mark on a wax seal. This impression, with as much blood as could be got from a pinprick, was then transferred to a wall. Such an explanation, although it appears to have eluded Watson at the time, would be child's play to today's Scene of Crime Officers. And teams of professionals 'lifting' prints, with volunteers combing an area inch by inch in finger-tip searches (bagging their finds) have augmented Holmes' crawling over the ground with his high-powered lens.

It's strange that we never hear of Doctor Watson in the laboratory, however. Given his presumed background, he could very quickly and easily dissect a body and extract a bullet, distinguishing between small entry and spread exit wounds. Although at that time he would not be able to identify the gun from which the bullet came but only its type. One of the earliest occasions when bullets were unarguably linked with a particular gun was in 1927, after the murder of a policeman, George Gutteridge, by Frederick Browne and William Kennedy. And it surely shouldn't have been necessary for Holmes to tell Watson about powder burns? These are present if the victim has been shot at close range but absent if the gunman fired from some distance away. The experience gained in treating the wounded in Afghanistan would tell Watson that. He should have been able to see for himself that William Kirwan, the Cunninghams' coachman in the Reigate Squire Adventure, wasn't shot by somebody very near him, a would-be Intruder (as they claimed). This apparent willingness of Watson to be instructed by Holmes may, however, be a ploy enabling him as a writer to pass on esoteric information in an interesting way to his readers, and not the result of something more suspect, such as not being a medical man at all!

The Doctor's knowledge of military arms and 'Khyber knives' would also have helped him to recognise what type of weapon had inflicted a fatal wound and, as a medical man, he could estimate the time of death with a reasonable degree of accuracy. Rigor mortis takes approximately twelve hours to be fully complete, lasts roughly the same amount of time and takes another twelve hours to disappear. It is on the subject of rigor mortis that Watson is for once given his head and remarks in 'The Resident Patient' about the hanged man Blessington, "I should say he has been dead about three hours, judging by the rigidity of the muscles." A more reliable method of estimating the time of death, however, is to consider body temperature. A corpse loses heat at the rate of between one and two degrees Fahrenheit per hour until it reaches the ambient or outside figure. Time of death is therefore arrived at by seeing how much heat has been lost compared to the known temperature of a living human body in normal circumstances. Watson was possibly aware of this, but when he wrote up the case probably stuck to rigor mortis as an estimation of the time of death because it was more familiar to the general public – who were avid readers of newspaper accounts of lurid murder cases.

Watson's experience as an army surgeon in terrain where more men died of fever than from any other cause should have given him the confidence to say whether a victim has died of disease, or been poisoned. The symptoms caused by some noxious substances are indistinguishable from those caused by natural illnesses. For example, the convulsions brought on by strychnine poisoning mimic those seen in cases of tetanus. Arsenic given in fatal quantities produces the same outward effect as gastro-enteritis, and even cholera. But one would have expected Watson to have had a head start over civilian doctors.

 Sherlock Holmes of course, with his all abiding interest in chemistry, must have been aware of the relatively simple reduction and precipitate tests for certain poisons (which Watson would also know how to do) and perhaps be more skilled than his colleague at performing the somewhat complicated test for arsenic in the tissues. This test was invented by James Marsh in 1836. But before this poisoners seemed to have it all their own way. Arsenic might be found in a drink offered to the victim, but unless it could also be found in the dead body this wasn't enough to convince a jury. However, although the Andaman Islander in *The Sign of Four* uses poisoned darts, and a retired colourman kills his wife and her lover with gas, Watson more or less avoided writing about these particular ways of committing a murder. Even if, as a doctor, he must have known all about them. However, he does report Holmes as citing Palmer and Wainwright who, according to Sherlock, were not only notorious poisoners but medical men "at the top of their profession." They weren't, of course. Sherlock is simply exaggerating for effect. The other great exception to not writing about poison is when Drebber is given a dose of it by Jefferson Hope in *A Study in Scarlet*, with pills Dr. Watson would have known exactly how to make up. And there were other ways in which jurisprudence could be used in suspected criminal cases. For example, Holmes uses his knowledge of cigar and cigarette ash to exonerate James McCarthy in 'The Boscombe Valley Mystery'. In 'The Resident Patient' he is able to show that the cigar stubs found in Blessington's room were of Dutch manufacture, whereas Blessington smoked Havanas. He had, therefore, not committed suicide but been murdered by men intent on revenge. So intent that they are willing for one of them to pose as a cataleptic and invade a respectable doctor's surgery. It is, however, always extremely difficult to distinguish tobacco deposits by concentrating on colour, or even texture, alone. Far better to analyse the chemical content of various 'weeds'. This depends on the soil in which the tobacco has been grown, and in any case American cigarettes had chemicals added to them. These were either in little pellets dispersed throughout the artefact or mixed directly with the tobacco to make them burn. This was not allowed in Britain, where instead the flammable agent was added to the paper.

Watson tells us that Holmes is also a skilful analyser of handwriting, giving evidence of such expertise as early as *The Sign of Four*. The idiosyncrasies of Thaddeus Sholto's hand, even when disguised as in his letter to Mary Morstan, are easily recognisable. And in 'The Man with the Twisted Lip' Holmes is able to see the difference between the use of a blotter, and ink which has been allowed to dry naturally. In the Greek Interpreter case Mycroft Holmes, said by Sherlock to be even more astute than he is, deduces that a letter has been written with a J pen, one with a broad-pointed nib, on royal cream paper by a middle-aged man with a weak constitution. Father and son, in the Reigate Squire Mystery, have written alternate words on a scrap of paper found between the finger and thumb of their murdered servant. Holmes is able to demonstrate this fact to Watson by discussing hereditary, or genetic, principles. He was also able to deduce that it was done so that, if caught, both men would have an equal share of blame for the crime. When it came to 'A Case of Identity' not only did Watson report that his friend was able to say (on first meeting her) that a deceived woman was a short-sighted typist, but he also proved on which typewriter the letters which took her in were typed: "I think of writing another little monograph some of these days on the typewriter and its relation to crime. It is a subject to which I have devoted some little attention. I have here four letters which purport to come from the missing man. They are all typewritten. In each case, not only are the 'e's' slurred and the 'r's' tail-less, but you will observe, if you care to use my magnifying lens, that the fourteen other characteristics to which I have alluded are there as well." In other words typewriters are as individual as handwriting, and 'Mr. Windibank' need not flatter himself he has got away with it, even if his behaviour isn't actionable. In addition to all this, Holmes can distinguish a man's trade by its effect on his physique. He is able to date documents, and can, like Wilde's Dorian Gray, identify perfumes.

Part of the charm of Watson's accounts of the investigations he shared with Holmes is that the two men are rarely in real danger. Even if they come pretty near it in 'The Devil's Foot'. It is only in subsequent pastiches and some films that they face the possibility of a grisly death. The villains in the original adventures are normally obvious, or very lightly disguised, and when caught usually come quietly. And, as is usual with other writers who have followed Watson, the person most suspected of the crime is innocent. Certain expressions appear in all the stories so that when they come round again the familiarity makes them sound comforting, rather like the present day catch phrases of comedians on radio and television. We feel we are on safe ground in such tales, not adrift in alien territory.

But if, instead of complaining about the paucity of his pension Watson had gone back to his old hospital, how much more useful he might have been to Holmes! Especially when applying that famous 'infallible test' Sherlock was so certain would supersede the usual tests for bloodstains: when resin from the guaiacum or *lignum vitae* tree (a native of the West Indies and South America) was mixed with alcohol and then added to the stain, together with a few drops of hydrogen peroxide dissolved in ether. This procedure, said Sherlock, "was very clumsy and uncertain." And microscopic examination "is valueless if the [blood] stains are a few hours old." His new test appeared to work on both new and old stains, and if it had been around earlier "hundreds of men now walking the earth…would long ago have paid the penalty of their crimes."

Watson makes the mistake, in 'The Priory School', of describing blood which has been around for a while as "bright red." But, says Holmes pettishly to his long-suffering helper in 'The Disappearance of Lady Frances Carfax', "A very pretty hash you have made of it, my dear Watson. I cannot at the moment recall any possible blunder which you have omitted. The total effect of your proceedings has been to give the alarm everywhere and yet to discover nothing." In 'A Case of Identity' he says, "You did not know where to look, and so you missed all that was important. I can never bring you to realise the importance of sleeves, the suggestiveness of thumb-nails, or the great issues that may hang from a bootlace." Which is tantamount to saying that, in his opinion, Watson's help in or out of any laboratory would have been worse than useless. But as Partha Basu points out in *The Curious Case of 221B: The Secret Notebooks of John H. Watson, MD*, a book kindly brought to my attention by Roger Johnson, Watson would have been quite justified in retorting: "It was I who tracked Lady Frances; it was I who discovered the Shlessingers, and their hold on her and the fact that they spirited her away to London. I did not raise any alarm with the Shlessingers or with Lady Frances because they had already left the Continent when I happened onto their trail. You, on the other hand, ignored my accurate deduction that the three were in London and not in Montpelier when you landed up in your ludicrous disguise..."

Holmes' insistence on "the importance of sleeves" and "the suggestiveness of thumb-nails" when trying to discover as much about a person as possible, including what work they do for a living, has led other writers to employ the same technique. Georges Simenon's Detective, Maigret, says he would have known whether a dead man was a cobbler or a tailor because "Doctor Paul would have told me. So would Moers." The doctor would do this "by studying the hands, the calluses, the deformations; Moers from the dust he'd have found in the clothes." Dust in the clothes is known as 'trace evidence', which can be found in every part of the body and its coverings: bringing to mind Edmond Locard's assertion that everything leaves its mark. Although 'The Blue Carbuncle' is about a robbery and not a murder, Watson's description of Holmes' study of a battered hat – the owner has "grizzled hair which he has had cut within the last few days, and which he anoints with lime cream" – is an example of the way in which trace evidence can be interpreted. Holmes, being Holmes, also uses the hat to discuss aspects of the man's character, his history, economic decline and general defects. In the last story of all recorded by Watson Holmes will again be occupied by someone's headgear, this time a cap. On it he will find hairs, dust, skin cells and, all importantly, glue. The murderer is a picture-framer.

Bodily markings, both natural and artificial, are also a useful tool in forensics. So the reader is not surprised to hear Holmes has written yet another monograph. This time on tattoos. These tell him something useful about the elderly pawnbroker in 'The Red-Headed League'. On one of the two occasions when Sherlock's brother Mycroft stirs himself enough (in 'The Greek Interpreter') to leave his office and the Diogenes Club, a place where no one is allowed to take any notice of anyone else and which he founded, the two siblings look out of the window and identify a billiard marker by some chalk marks over the man's waistcoat pocket. They then go on, in a kind of friendly rivalry and to demonstrate just how clever Mycroft really is, to talk about "a very small, dark fellow with his hat pushed back and several packages under his arm."

They identify him between them as a recently discharged non-commissioned officer who has served in

India with the Royal Artillery and is now a widower. There is some disagreement about the number of children he has. Sherlock says one, but Mycroft opts for more than one because the man is carrying a rattle, obviously meant for a babe in arms, and a picture book more suitable to an older child. An air of authority marks the man out as more than a private. And there is no mistaking his military bearing. The way he wears his hat, says Holmes, reveals that the skin on one side of his face is lighter than on the other. Is Sherlock about to make the same mistake he did about Watson when they first met and he told him he had come from the tropics? Like Watson's wrists, this man's brow is fair, while any visible skin is tanned. But that would not prove unequivocally where he had been stationed. However, the Doctor is certainly repeating some of the ideas from *A Study in Scarlet*.

But this piece of entertaining and satisfying interplay between two clever men, with clues which when explained show how easy it all is, goes a long way towards solving the mystery why such an iconic pair, or in this case a trio, as Watson the writer, Sherlock the sleuth and Mycroft the secret civil servant still have such a hold over us all. The ex-soldier is in deep mourning. Perhaps having such a very young infant means his wife died in childbirth? If she were still alive he would probably not be doing his own shopping. He hasn't the 'cavalry stride', but his weight tells against his being a sapper so it must be the Artillery. In any case, he is wearing his 'ammunition boots'. In the end we think we have worked it out all by ourselves, even if Watson is (or pretends to be) completely baffled.

He has an interest in pathology, as befits a doctor and in 'The Boscombe Valley Mystery', first speculates on whether or not a young man could be innocent in spite of the damning evidence against him. Might not the nature of the murdered man's injuries reveal something to a medic? He rings for a newspaper and reads a verbatim account of the inquest. He then tells the reader that "It was stated in the surgeon's deposition that the posterior third of the left parietal bone and the left half of the occipital bone had been shattered by a heavy blow from a blunt instrument. I marked the spot on my own head. Clearly such a blow must have been struck from behind. That was to some extent in favour of the accused, as when seen quarrelling he was face to face with his father." Perhaps the older man turned away just as the blow fell? Was talk of "a rat" evidence of delirium? Victims of heavy blows to the head did not normally become delirious.

So the Doctor reasons, in the best traditions of the discipline. It seems he can think for himself and does know where to look, in spite of Holmes' contemptuous attitude. An interest in pathology, especially in connection with crime, *would* make him aware of the importance of thumbnails. Given the number of times Holmes reprimands his friend, and his patronising comment, "You are doing remarkably well," is Sherlock Holmes perhaps compensating for a deep sense of inferiority in himself? The snubs given to Watson in the early part of *The Valley of Fear*, as well as those in 'The Disappearance of Lady Frances Carfax', are sufficient to make the reader think so. And what about this from 'The Solitary Cyclist': "Your hiding place, my dear Watson, was very faulty. You should have been behind the hedge; then you would have a clear view of this interesting person. As it is you were some hundreds of yards away and can tell me even less than Miss Smith. You really have done remarkably badly." It's enough to make any red-blooded man throw in the towel.

Chapter Seven: On Being the Historian of this Bunch

In spite of such a devastating attack by Holmes as we saw in the last chapter, Watson continued to be a willing recorder of their *Adventures* together. At the beginning of 'The Five Orange Pips', an investigation which appears to have taken place in 1887 and some time before the episode of 'The Solitary Cyclist', he tells us he has been looking over his notes for 1882-1890 before deciding to publish this particular tale; but, prior to attempting any enlargement of his role as the recorder of Holmes' triumphs (and occasional failures), perhaps it's time to look into some little mysteries of his own.

Readers have been led to believe Watson's first experience of detection began in *A Study in Scarlet*, in which an American hunter takes revenge on two Mormon Elders for abducting the girl he loved. But in what year did the former 'Sergeant of Marines' appear in Baker Street with news that there had been murder done? We know from internal evidence that it was the fourth of March, and that he brought a letter from Inspector Gregson telling Holmes about the "bad business" in Lauriston Gardens. In that case, when exactly did Watson get home from Afghanistan? When, precisely, did he land at Portsmouth Jetty? How long did it take him to 'gravitate' to London? He stayed for "some time" at the hotel in the Strand. But was it long enough to account for what is beginning to seem a significant gap in his history? It took him "a day or two" to settle into Baker Street once he'd decided to share lodgings with Holmes, and perhaps was not there long before *A Study in Scarlet* intervened.

This might mean that the unfortunate Doctor, if after all he was sent to the wrong Base Hospital, spent even more time in Peshawar trying to recover his health than we thought. He may not have arrived in England until more than a year after the Battle of Maiwand. So can one say with any certainty that the Jefferson Hope murders took place in 1881, or should we be looking at something a little more suspicious? The three-act play, *Angels of Darkness,* already mentioned in Chapter One, suggests that we should. Much of the material in it appears in Part 11 of *A Study in Scarlet* ("The Flower of Utah") which had to be padded out to the required length. Was the Doctor already practising for his literary and theatrical life? If we are to believe the events of the play, Dr. Watson is more than just a ladies' man with 'experience of women' which extended 'over many nations and three separate continents.' He has either married some other woman before meeting Mary Morstan, or else heartlessly jilted her at the final curtain. But, as noted earlier, the play was never published. A wise precaution, since the 'other woman' is Lucy Ferrier, the unfortunate victim of the Mormon marriage in *A Study in Scarlet*! Besides, Watson without Holmes wouldn't have gone down at all well with the readers of *The Strand Magazine* or, come to that, theatre-goers.

It is problematical, of course, to accept that Watson was ever in America after his exit from Afghanistan – however much one would like to do so. Someone as emaciated as he was, suffering from the effects of fever, a shoulder wound or, in another of his accounts, a bullet in the leg, couldn't be expected to make such a journey in the days before air travel – and perhaps not even then. But could he have been there in the summer of 1878? Did his course at Netley begin later than he made it appear, and stretch way beyond November? He tells us he was late in getting to India. So late that he missed the beginning of hostilities in Afghanistan and had to find his regiment for himself. So, however, did many others "in the same situation." But, although the campaign began suddenly, it wasn't that much of a surprise. Troops stationed in India had been put on alert for some weeks, and in any case conditions in that area were always volatile. Would a large number of men be late joining their regiments? Maybe, especially if they were coming out from England. Perhaps here we have to give Watson the benefit of the doubt. The implication is that, although he was late, he wasn't that late.

More mysteries present themselves later on when Watson first begins writing for *The Strand Magazine*. In 'A Scandal in Bohemia' he says, "I had seen little of Holmes lately. My marriage had drifted us away from each other. My own complete happiness, and the home-centred interests which rise up around the man who first finds himself master of his own establishment, were sufficient to absorb all my attention." It is 1888 and Watson has also "returned to civil practice." He appears to have married Mary Morstan soon after the end of the investigation into *The Sign of Four*: which, on the evidence of the number of pearls she shows Holmes when they first meet, would seem to have taken place in 1887, so when and where did he do his *first* stint of civil practice? Not, surely, in Baker Street when he was still so poorly and the place stank of chemicals? Since he has been careful to tell us he went straight from university to Netley and from there to Afghanistan he couldn't have been in civil practice before (or in between) those two events either.

And what about some of his other statements? When he told Holmes (in 'Shoscombe Old Place') that his summer quarters were once in Berkshire he was speaking of something which has a strong military flavour. Troops, at home and abroad, habitually went into summer and winter quarters. Major-General Roberts for example, after a skirmish in the Khost Valley, and finding that his force was too small to hold both that and the Kuram Valley against the Afghans, evacuated the former and went into winter quarters. This had already been done in the Khyber region because of the enormous difficulties of trying to take Kabul before the snows set in and blocked the Pass. But, for the same reasons that Watson couldn't have been in civil practice before going to Afghanistan, so he couldn't be in summer quarters either then or – as a discharged combatant – when he got back. So was Watson simply referring to his training as an assistant surgeon in the army, part of which took place at Aldershot during the five or six months he was at Netley?

With regard to the initial contact with Holmes, can the plaque on a wall near the Pathology Laboratory at Bart's be correct when it reads 'At this place New Year's Day 1881 were spoken these deathless words "You have been in Afghanistan, I perceive," by Mr Sherlock Holmes in greeting to John H. Watson at their first meeting? There has been some confusion among commentators about the date on which the Battle of Maiwand took place. Jack Tracy and June Thomson initially opt for the twenty-seventh of June, which was obviously a mistake. Other sources mention men returning from battle on the *morning* of July 27th, confusing them with General Burrows' reconnoitring force sent out the day before. The Court Circular published in *The Times* for August 18th 1882 records the date as 24th July 1880. However more reliable sources, for example Leigh Maxwell in *My God! Maiwand* and Richard Stacpoole-Ryding in *Maiwand: The Last Stand of the 66th (Berkshire) Regiment in Afghanistan, 1880,* give the true date: the afternoon of July 27th 1880. Roberts' victorious engagement with Ayub Khan's Army took place on the first of September. Taking the twenty-seventh of July and September 1st 1880 as a starting point, there are cogent reasons why Watson couldn't have made up his mind to change his way of life until at least early January 1881. He says of his stay in hospital that he only rallied enough to walk about the wards and to bask a little on the verandah before being struck down by fever. In which case he was lucky to be alive at all. The area around Peshawar was known to European troops as the valley of death, and those who went there couldn't wait to leave. He has either exaggerated the length of his illness, his period of recovery and his stays at various venues before being introduced to Holmes, or the supposed date of their meeting should be considerably advanced.

Even if we accept that he muddled up the names of the base hospitals and *was* one of the eighteen invalids who left Karachi in the *Orontes,* roughly six weeks after the Kandahar Garrison was relieved by Roberts, and arrived in England in the middle of November 1880, he would still have to go some to meet Sherlock on the first of January 1881. For example, how long after he docked at Portsmouth Jetty did he stay in Hampshire? 'Gravitating' to London implies a period of doubt about what to do next, and his "comfortless, meaningless existence" in that hotel in the Strand appears to have lasted for quite a while. It is only when he realises that he is living above his means and feels the need to retrench that he uses the word "soon". And even healthy, unscathed combatants who took part in the military engagement at Maiwand didn't get back to barracks in Britain until February 18th, 1881.

However, it makes for better 'theatre' to fix the

meeting between the two men, who were to become such famous colleagues in the fighting of crime, for New Year's Day. The laboratories were empty, apart from Sherlock, and the streets thronged with people. January 1st did not become a bank holiday until 1971, and in the nineteenth century most people worked on Saturday mornings. Was 'young Stamford' on his way out to lunch after finishing a morning's stint as a dresser, or perhaps a newly qualified doctor, at Bart's when he met Watson? Were the streets crowded with Saturday afternoon shoppers?

For anyone who thinks, in the light of all Watson's difficulties as a soldier and as a civilian, that it is more likely he did meet Holmes a year later than he said, it's useful to know that, in 1882, January 1st fell on a Sunday. Sherlock, when the mood for action was on him, wouldn't care what day, or what time of day, it was and may have obtained permission to conduct his own private enquiries into cadavers and/or bloodstains on Sunday, as well as Saturday, afternoons. This permission, once Holmes was accepted as a visitor, would not be difficult to get. Is it safe to assume that, unless stirred by something really exciting, he would be quite unobtrusive; even if Stamford – a man who obviously keeps his ear close to the ground – spotted the dead-body beating? But, if the laboratories were closed on Sunday, Holmes may have preferred to inspect what became their mutual lodgings on that day. It would mean less chance of his work being interrupted if he went about other business when laboratories were closed! Sunday may also have suited the landlady better. It took a very short time for them to settle in, and to arrange their possessions. But in Watson's words the two men *gradually* adapted to their new life. There were many occasions when Holmes worked hard at something mysterious. But for *days on end* there were "intervals of torpor", when he lay on the sofa not uttering a word or moving a muscle. *Weeks went by* as Watson, whose health forbade him venturing out "unless the weather was exceptionally genial," wondered what on earth Sherlock could be doing for a living. Taken with all the other imponderables, the weather's keeping Watson in points to the possibility of the season being autumn or winter. But fixing his meeting with Holmes for the first day of 1881 allows very little flexibility when trying to sort out a timetable for him after Maiwand.

In a 1948 article for *The Baker Street Journal* W. S. Baring-Gould opted for March 4th 1882 as the date when the investigation into the murder of Enoch Drebber took place. But by 1962 he appears to have changed his mind, perhaps because another man with a scholarly interest in Holmes and Watson, Ernest Bloomfield Zeisler, the same man who suggested Watson was removed from his brigade while in Afghanistan because he had syphilis, argued strongly for the earlier date. However, 1882 fits Watson's own account of his troubles more plausibly than that he met up with Holmes barely five months after being so badly wounded in Afghanistan and so seriously affected by fever. Perhaps a compromise is in order? Did he meet Holmes in 1881 but not as early as New Year's Day? The weather could have been just as inclement in November or December as in January for Watson not to risk exacerbating the pain of his injuries by venturing out of doors. But the period between autumn 1881 and spring 1882 was perhaps long enough to account for the time it might take to become friendly enough with such a solitary creature as Holmes to be invited to take part in one of his investigations.

Dating this first Adventure, however, is difficult for other reasons. In 1881 March 4th fell on Friday. But, when the pair leave Lauriston Gardens after viewing Drebber's corpse, Holmes tells Watson he is in a hurry to get to a concert. He is anxious to hear the famous violinist Wilma Norman-Neruda (Mrs. Charles Hallé). But Madame Norman-Neruda gave recitals only on Monday evenings and Saturday afternoons. Her concert on Saturday the fifth of March 1881 was the last of the season, starting as usual at 3 p.m. *The Standard,* according to Watson, wrote that the two murdered men (Drebber and Stangerson) "bade adieu to their landlady upon *Tuesday*, the 4th inst." [My italics]. They were last seen later that evening standing on the platform at Euston Station waiting for a late train to Liverpool. The note from Tobias Gregson to Holmes said that Drebber's body was discovered by a passing constable [John Rance] in Lauriston Gardens at 2 the following morning. Lestrade reported that Stangerson was killed in Halliday's Private Hotel, Little George Street, at six in the morning the following day, and his body not found until two hours later. He complicates matters further by saying that the two Americans were seen on Euston Station on *Monday* the 3rd of March. But the dates given by the newspaper and Lestrade are obviously wrong if the Jefferson Hope Investigation was conducted in 1881 or in 1882. March 4th fell on Tuesday in 1884 (a leap year) and March 3rd on Monday in 1890, for example. It almost seems as if Watson delayed writing up his account until very early in 1885 and used last year's calendar (still hanging on the wall) to date it!

In 'The Resident Patient' Watson says that he can't be sure of the exact date when this particular investigation got under way, but that it must have been towards the end of the first year he shared lodgings with Holmes. He mentions "boisterous October weather" and, with his health shaken, being afraid "to face the keen autumn wind." It is becoming more and more obvious that he did not meet Holmes until much later than New Year's Day, 1881. His first year in Baker Street began towards the end of October 1881, the Enoch Drebber affair took place five months later and Watson was still feeling the effect of his wounds seven months after that. He says that the Speckled Band case took place at the beginning of April 1883, "in the *early days* [my italics] of my association with Holmes, when we were sharing rooms as bachelors." This also implies that he took up lodgings in Baker Street considerably later than January 1st 1881.

There is, incidentally, a further puzzle of a financial sort. Watson's wound pension was temporary, judging by his remark that he was given nine months by a paternal government to recover his health. Wounded officers who were expected to return to service were put on full-pay for a short time, then went onto half-pay and back to full-pay once they were deemed fit for duty. But Watson's health was "irretrievably ruined". He was not expected to return to his regiment. So what did he live on when his pension stopped? Mycroft Holmes asserts, in 'The Greek Interpreter', that he hears of Sherlock everywhere (presumably at work and in The Diogenes Club since he apparently goes nowhere else) after Watson got him into print. White Mason, one of the policemen in *The Valley of Fear*, says jovially, "Come along, Dr. Watson, and when the time comes we'll all hope to find a place in your book." Later in the same investigation Jack Douglas tells Watson that he has heard of him: "You are the historian of this bunch." Holmes also speaks humorously of an early case "before my biographer came to glorify me." Books have been in the Doctor's sights from the beginning. At the end of what is generally accepted as their first investigation together, Holmes remarks that the result of all their "Study in Scarlet" is to get the police a testimonial. To which Watson replies, "Never mind, I have all the facts in my journal, and the public shall know them." Perhaps *The Strand Magazine* paid him enough not to worry about when his pension would come to an end, although he was still talking about it when he published 'Shoscombe Old Place' in April, 1927.

But maybe he did begin practising as a civilian doctor before his marriage to Mary Morstan, a marriage sometimes said not to have taken place in 1887/88 but 1889 – although that date too is something of a mystery. We have already noted how difficult it would have been to see the sick in the crowded sitting room in Baker Street. But there was nothing to stop Watson hiring a consulting room somewhere else once he was well enough. Readers are inclined to assume that his sorties with Holmes, including the writing up of them, occupied his every waking moment. But could these investigations have been a means of relaxation for him in between treating patients? We have already seen, in 'The Five Orange Pips', how Watson is glancing over his notes because he can't decide, not for the first time, which case to put before his readers. There's plenty of choice. But some have already been in the public domain, although we are not told exactly when or where. Other investigations don't offer enough scope to display Holmes' unique qualities "which it is the object of these papers to illustrate." The Doctor finds some cases comic, others tragic, but 'The Speckled Band' "presented more singular features than any other." There are those of us who might find all this decision-making stressful, but it's meat and drink to Holmes' faithful scribe. In addition to his lengthy accounts, he strews titles of other investigations about in order to present Sherlock as an even greater detective, and indicates he is searching through piles of manuscripts to show how much the man was in demand. It is success which brings rewards and clients, and how very exciting it all is!

As Sherlock says, tossing the Daily Telegraph to one side and for once paying a surely gratified Watson a qualified compliment in 'The Copper Beeches', "It is pleasant to me to observe, Watson, that...in these little records of our cases which you have been good enough to draw up, and, I am bound to say, occasionally to embellish, you have given prominence not so much to the many *causes célèbres* and sensational trials in which I have figured, but rather to those incidents which may have been trivial in themselves, but which have given room for those faculties of deduction and of logical synthesis which I have made my special province."

Watson, however, has to admit to the sensationalism of some of his accounts, laying himself open to some nit-picking by Holmes, who says his scribe errs in lending colour and life to his statements instead of placing on record "that severe reasoning from cause to effect which is really the only notable feature about the thing." One is glad to hear the poor man make a protest: "It seems to me that I have done you full justice in the matter" before listening to yet another lecture. After all, considering what was going on in Victorian England, he does seem to have avoided too much of what might be termed sensational. Of the cases he has put before the public, the majority deal with deception of some kind. The next largest groups deal with robbery or fraud. Three are about blackmail, and include one which could be termed sensational if we accept that Black Peter's being skewered with his own harpoon comes into that category. The violence for the most part is confined to the Andaman Islander, who does for Bartholomew Sholto with a poison dart expelled from a blow-pipe. But it is the revenge killings which show most the element deplored by Holmes. Drebber and Stangerson die respectively from poisoning and stab wounds and Jim Browner batters his wife and her lover to death on a boat in New Brighton. Other out-of-the way investigations, such as 'The Lion's Mane', 'The Devil's Foot' and 'The Sussex Vampire', shock because these events are so unfamiliar. The Doctor, however, seems at first to have taken his friend's strictures to heart. Even though he says, in the rather gruesome tale called 'The Cardboard Box', "It is, however, unfortunately impossible to entirely separate the sensational from the criminal, and a chronicler is left in the dilemma that he must either sacrifice details which are essential to his statement, and so give a false impression of the problem, or he must use matter which chance, and not choice, has provided him with." But, in choosing cases that illustrate the remarkable mental qualities of his friend Holmes, he says that he tries as far as possible to avoid being too sensational.

By the time 'The Resident Patient' was written, featuring the death by hanging of a respectable doctor's tenant, Watson appears to have changed his mind. The memoirs have also become "somewhat incoherent." We are aware of another of his problems in 'The Naval Treaty'. Some investigations deal with matters of such importance, and implicate so many top people, that they cannot be made public for years - and the new century will have come before a particular story ('The Second Stain') can be safely told. Watson is true to his word. It wasn't published until

1904.

He takes up his pen with a heavy heart to relate the supposed death of Sherlock Holmes in 'The Final Problem', determined to make "a clear statement of his [Moriarty's] career." Injudicious champions, including Moriarty's possibly older brother (who Watson identifies as a colonel, the younger brother being, according to what was said by Holmes to Inspector MacDonald in *The Valley of Fear*, a station master in the west of England), were attempting to clear Moriarty of his crimes by making an attack on Holmes. Something the Doctor could not possibly countenance. But what he feared most didn't actually happen. Holmes returns to the land of the living to solve (among other cases) the mystery of the man who, by using a dead animal, fakes his own death by fire. Sherlock says to him, "By the way, what was it you put into the wood-pile besides your old trousers? A dead dog, or rabbits, or what? You won't tell? Dear me, how very unkind of you! Well, well, I dare say that a couple of rabbits would account both for the blood and for the charred ashes. If ever you write an account, Watson, you can make rabbits serve your turn." Encouraged, the Doctor decides he *will* write-up the case. The result is 'The Norwood Builder'. As usual, Holmes declines to be recognised as the one who has solved the mystery, telling the police detective, "Instead of being ruined you will find your reputation has been enormously advanced. Just make a few alterations in that report which you were writing and they will understand how hard it is to throw dust in the eyes of Inspector Lestrade." To this the reply is "And you don't want your name to appear?" Holmes does not. The work is its own reward, and "Perhaps I shall get the credit also at some distant day when I permit my zealous historian to lay out his foolscap once more – eh,

Watson?"

Holmes is extremely interested in codes and, at the end of the investigation into the 'Dancing Men', remarks to the Doctor, "I think that I have fulfilled my promise of giving you something unusual for your note-book." This is a copy of the code he has cracked and used to lure a murderer into his net. We can be sure Watson not only used but treasured it. In 'His Last Bow', when Holmes and Watson are heavily involved with spies, John Buchan has his hero, Richard Hannay, strongly interested in codes: and most of his chapters labelled as 'Adventures'. Hannay, however, makes a point of saying he is "no Sherlock Holmes." Obviously not. But Watson certainly seems to have provided the inspiration and Buchan is obviously acknowledging this.

In a long preamble to 'The Solitary Cyclist' Watson explains again how he makes his choice of story for publication, and seems to have written up 'Black Peter' simply so that he can reveal to his readers the startling fact that Holmes walked through the streets of London carrying "a huge barbed-headed spear." But in 'Charles Augustus Milverton' he is again saying that it would have been impossible, even with the utmost discretion and reticence, to make the facts made public any earlier. Now the principal person was beyond human law; and Watson would tell the tale in such a way that no one could be injured by it. Even so, this ultra-cautious writer will suppress some facts and hopes that the readers will excuse him if he doesn't mention the date, or anything else which would enable them to trace the occurrence. Buyers of *The Strand Magazine* were being skilfully prepared for a really horrendous crime – blackmail. And Watson was letting himself off the hook by not providing too much detail.

By the time 'The Golden Pince-Nez' was written

Watson appears bogged down by "three massive manuscript volumes." He is again studying his notes for investigations not only interesting but able to do justice to Holmes' "peculiar powers." In 'The Singular Experience of Mr. John Scott Eccles' Holmes says, "I suppose, Watson, we must look upon you as a man of letters" and asks how the Doctor would define the word 'grotesque'. In 'The Devil's Foot' Watson reveals the perennial problem he has when it comes to pleasing Holmes, even though the detective has told him (in 'The Man with the Twisted Lip') "Oh, a trusty companion is always of use; and a chronicler still more so." But Sherlock's inconsistent aversion to publicity has caused Watson to lay "very few" of his records before the public lately. Holmes, however, has now sent a telegram suggesting he publish 'The Devil's Foot' because it was "the strangest case I have handled."

Sherlock was also not averse to the publication of the singular facts connected with Professor Presbury. But things were soon back to normal when "for the tenth time in as many years" Watson begs leave to reveal the facts behind 'The Illustrious Client', a successful investigation which he calls "in some ways, the supreme moment of my friend's career." This may not be too much of an exaggeration. At the end of the case when Miss Violet de Merville, the supposed daughter of General de Merville "of Khyber fame", has been saved from a disastrous marriage to the "Austrian murderer", Baron Gruner, Watson sees Sir James Damery drive away from Baker Street in a carriage emblazoned with a distinctive Coat-of-Arms. It was Sir James (who "has rather a reputation for arranging delicate matters which are to be kept out of the papers") who commissioned Holmes to prevent the marriage, but he has already made it plain that he was only an emissary. Now the armorial bearings glimpsed by an astonished Watson show that it wasn't General de Merville who sent him to Holmes. Full of awe, Watson goes back upstairs and bursts into the sitting-room he used to share with Sherlock. He has found out who the client really is! Before he can utter more than two words the detective holds up a restraining hand and says, "It is a loyal friend and chivalrous gentleman. Let that now and forever be enough for us." Poor Watson. Robbed of his moment of revelation and burdened forever with a secret he cannot share, surely he felt that he would never get anything past such a friend?

Speculation became rife among readers of *The Strand Magazine* that the owner of the Coat-of-Arms on the carriage was royal. The Illustrious Client wishing to save Miss Violet de Merville was King Edward V11. But it is hard to think of him as a loyal friend to an old soldier, especially someone he may have cuckolded. It's taken ten years for Watson to persuade Holmes to let him make the story public. By that time Edward was dead (which is perhaps why Holmes said, "It can't hurt now") and George V was on the throne. At the time of the investigation Miss de Merville was "of age," (that is, over twenty-one) and "a "lovely, innocent girl" born round about 1881, when Edward was forty years old and Prince of Wales. Although a rake, however, if he was nothing more than a good friend to an old soldier then rescuing the man's daughter from Baron Gruner may have been one of the first acts of his short reign, as well as a disinterested one.

As for Watson, 'The Blanched Soldier' witnesses the worm turning at last when, after years of being told he panders to the popular taste with his superficial accounts, the exasperated medic bursts out with "Try it yourself, Holmes!" But it's not as easy as it seems, and there are definite echoes of *A Study in Scarlet* during an interview Sherlock has with Mr. James M. Dodd, who is "From South Africa, I perceive." Holmes is profiting from Watson's first literary effort. But he discovers that one cannot stick simply to bald facts and figures; it is also necessary to interest the reader. However, one thing does irk Sherlock. He has to show his hand in telling his own story. It turns out that over the years he has continually concealed links in the chain of investigations from Watson, making it very difficult, as we suspected, for the Doctor to appear other than dim. Small wonder he seems so thick at times if vital information is being withheld from him.

In 'The Veiled Lodger' Watson has "a mass of material at my command." He has been with Holmes for seventeen of the twenty-three years the Detective was in active practice, and yet again the problem is one of choice. This, however, was the last time he referred to his difficulties as an historian, being content to simply record what happened in the final published account of his *Adventures* with Holmes: 'Shoscombe Old Place'. He still manages however, at over seventy, to interest the reader right from the start. Holmes is bending over a low-power microscope. He straightens up and looks round triumphantly. "It is glue, Watson. Unquestionably it is glue." The wheel has come full circle. Holmes is as excited as when he discovered the test for bloodstains in *A Study in Scarlet*.

Chapter Eight: On Restricting the Contents of a Brain-Attic

After Holmes deduces he has been in Afghanistan, and just before the pair embark on their first thrilling Adventure together, Watson makes the mistake of comparing his new friend to Dupin, saying, "I had no idea that such individuals did exist outside of stories." Sherlock's reply to this is that, in his opinion, "Dupin was a very inferior fellow. That trick of his of breaking into his friends' thoughts with an apropos remark after a quarter of an hour's silence is really very showy and superficial." While Holmes concedes that Dupin had some talent for analysis, "he was by no means such a phenomenon as Poe appeared to imagine."

The American writer Edgar Allan Poe was born in Boston in 1809. His detective has as his Watson an almost completely gullible friend who writes up the narratives of his investigations and is always flatteringly amazed at their outcome. Dupin continually produces a solution to each mystery, each time with a triumphant flourish. One which both surprises and satisfies his faithful amanuensis. Undeterred, however, by Holmes' dismissal of the man, Watson tries again with Gaboriau and asks, "Does Lecoq come up to your idea of a detective?"

Emile Gaboriau, novelist and pioneer of detective fiction, was born in the small village of Saujon in the French district of *Charente-Maritime* on November 9th, 1832. He sprang to fame in 1866 with *L'Affaire Lerouge,* in which a young policeman played the part of an amateur detective. This character, M. Lecoq, was based on Eugene Francois Vidocq (1775-1837) whose *Les Vrais Memoirs de Vidocq* were a curious mixture of fact and fiction by a man who began as a thief and then became a high-ranking police official in Paris. A certain villainous Lecoq had appeared in

Paul Féval's *Les Habits Noirs* series of books and this may have also influenced Gaboriau, who worked as a journalist for Féval and quietly appropriated the name for himself: giving it to an upholder of the law rather than to someone who was not. This time, however, Sherlock is seriously annoyed. "Lecoq was a miserable bungler. He had only one thing to recommend him and that was his energy. That book made me positively ill. The question was how to identify an unknown prisoner. I could have done it in twenty-four hours. Lecoq took six months or so. It might be made a text-book for detectives to teach them what to avoid."

Poor Watson feels so indignant at this treatment of two of his favourite fictional detectives that he has to walk away and gaze out of the window for a few minutes to calm down. Holmes will later break into his thoughts in much the same way as Dupin so his strictures do seem somewhat unfair. However, it must be admitted that, compared to Dupin's tortuous way of extrapolating the thought processes of *his* Watson, Sherlock's exposition of the visit by his colleague to the Wigmore Street Post Office, and of Watson's musings on General Gordon and Henry Ward Beecher, are a model of clarity.

But by the end of *A Study in Scarlet* the university-educated ex-army surgeon will show that he doesn't read only detective novels. He remembers his Latin, an essential requirement in those days for entry to university. Immediately after telling Holmes (who is complaining that the police will, as usual, get all the credit for solving the case) that he intends eventually to reveal all, Watson continues, "In the meantime you must make yourself contented by the consciousness of success, like the Roman miser –*Populus me sibilat, at mihi plaudo/Ipse domi simul ac nummos contemplar in arca.*" [The people hiss me, but I applaud myself as I count the money in my strongbox at home]

Watson also shows, by not turning a hair or asking for a translation when quotations are thrown at him, that he is familiar with French and German read in the original. But it seems hardly fair to blame him if he doesn't always get the foreign-language quotations right. After all, he's only telling us what Holmes said...[1] "*Il n'y a pas des sots si incommodes que ceux qui ont de l'esprit!*" [There are no fools as troublesome as those who have some wit] carols Sherlock, when describing Athelney Jones in *The Sign of Four* before hitting Watson with another quotation, this time in German: "I shall study the great Jones's methods and listen to his not too delicate sarcasms. *Wir sind gewohnt dass die Menschen verhöhnen was sie nicht verstehen.* [We are used to the fact that people make fun of the things they don't understand] Goethe is always pithy."

At the conclusion of the investigation Holmes feels compelled once more to break into German. After agreeing with the Doctor that he alternates "fits of splendid energy and vigour" with moods when he is "as limp as a rag" he says, "I often think of those lines of old Goethe: *Schade dass die Natur nur einen Mensch aus dir schuf, denn zum würdigen Mann war und zum Schelmen der Stoff.*" [It is too bad nature made you just one man, since there was material to make a worthy man and a jester]

Johann Wolfgang von Goethe (1749-1832) poet, polymath and amateur artist, was born in Frankfurt and studied law at the universities of Leipzig and Strasbourg. He became a member of the *Sturm und Drang* Movement, which believed in German art and individual creative

---

[1] I am indebted to Roger Johnson for this observation

genius, and wrote a number of books influenced by, and influencing, the Romantic Movement. His sentimental novel of unrequited love, *The Sorrows of Werther*, made him famous throughout Europe. It was so totally subjective, rebellious against authority – and obsessed with the quest for a degree of joy humanly unobtainable. A visit to Italy quickened Goethe's interest in Classical Literature but later, after he entered the service of Duke Karl August, Duke of Weimar as a kind of 'prime minister', he became involved in the science of Political Economy, producing several books on the subject.

Still on a somewhat ethereal plane, on one occasion Holmes is discussing some workers coming out of a ship yard by the Thames. "Dirty looking rascals, but I suppose everyone has some little immortal spark concealed about them. You would not think it to look at them. There is no *a priori* probability about it. A strange enigma is man!" Bringing Winwood Reade, the author of the nineteenth century shocker *The Martyrdom of Man*, into play in the same way as he did earlier he continues, "While the individual man is an insoluble puzzle, in the aggregate he becomes a mathematical certainty." But Watson has already in *The Sign of Four* passed up the opportunity to study Winwood Reade. However, he remarks that someone – he can't quite remember who – describes man as "a soul concealed in an animal."

Knowing that, in spite of an assumed off-hand attitude, his friend appreciates genuine praise, Watson goes over the top at the end of the investigation into the Red-Headed League saying, "You are a benefactor of the race." Holmes' (misquoted) reply to this piece of fulsomeness is *"L'homme c'est rien- l'oeuvre c'est tout,'* [The man is nothing, the work everything] as Gustave Flaubert wrote to George

Sand."

Flaubert, a French novelist whose notorious account of an adulterous woman, *Madame Bovary,* made him a household name, entered Parisian literary circles in 1840 at the age of nineteen. Six years later he went to live in Rouen and stayed there for the rest of his life. 'George Sand', born Amandine Aurore Lucie Dupin, was no female French detective but a prolific writer of basically autobiographical books. Married at eighteen, she deserted her husband, M. Dudevant, and went to Paris – where she had a number of love affairs with well-known writers and musicians, notably de Musset and Chopin. Her first novel, *Indiana,* published in 1832, dealt with a woman's right to be independent and was followed by others in a similar vein. Two years after her affair with Chopin ended she retired to Nobant in Central France with plenty of opportunity to write and receive letters.

At the conclusion of the investigation into the wrongs of the much deceived Miss Mary Sutherland, Holmes remarks to Watson, "You may remember the old Persian saying, 'There is danger for him who taketh the tiger cub, and danger also for whoso snatches a delusion from a woman.' There is as much sense in Hafiz as in Horace, and as much knowledge of the world." We don't know whether or not either of them read Persian, although Holmes may have a smattering of the language. He is briefly mentioned by Watson as having travelled in Persia. But Hafiz (Shams al-Din Muhammad, c.1326-1390) was a lyric poet who was born in Shiraz and taught in a dervish college there. His collection of short poems, known as the *Diwan*, are satires on his fellow dervishes – who could be whirling, dancing or howling depending on their bent – and also a celebration of the hedonistic pleasures of life. This last is a little surprising, as Holmes appears to derive most of *his* pleasure in life from the intellectual content of his work. But perhaps this is yet another example of his ambivalence. Like the cocaine, the tobacco in the slipper, the doctoring in place of Watson and (in spite of a shrinking- violet attitude to publicity) allowing him to write up at least some of their investigations. However, the quotation hasn't been found in Hafiz, nor yet anywhere else. The bracketing together by Holmes of the two poets (Hafiz with Horace) may simply mean that we can learn as much from the middle eastern civilisations as we can from Rome and Greece.[2]

In the old soldier's first published investigation together Watson whiles away the time waiting for Holmes by "stolidly puffing at my pipe and skipping over the pages of Henri Murger's *Scènes de la Vie de Bohème*." Bohemians were gypsies popularly supposed to have come to France from Bohemia in 1427 and camped outside Paris. Refused entry to the city, they were lodged in Saint-Denis. A *bohème* was a wanderer who lived by his wits and had no settled habits or home. It was also a slang term applied to literary men and artists living loose and irregular lives, existing by what they could get for nothing and what they could earn by cunning. Murger, who studied painting in Paris, had first-hand experience of such a life. The book mentioned by Watson was published in 1848 when the author was twenty-six, and is more properly a collection of short pieces which had previously appeared in various newspapers. It became a consistent bestseller during the nineteenth century and was used by Puccini and by Leoncavallo as the basis for their operas, both called *La Bohème* and produced in the eighteen-nineties. Watson says, in 'The Musgrave Ritual', "The rough-and-tumble

---

[2] Again, I am indebted to Roger Johnson for this suggestion

work in Afghanistan, coming on the top of a natural bohemianism of disposition, has made me rather more lax than befits a medical man." He also remarks that the house where Nathan Garrideb lived "was not a collection of residential flats, but rather the abode of Bohemian bachelors." He insists, however, that he isn't as Bohemian as Holmes "Who keeps his cigars in the coal-scuttle, his tobacco in the toe end of a Persian slipper, and his unanswered correspondence transfixed by a jack-knife into the very centre of his wooden mantelpiece."

Watson regards as ultra-bohemian Holmes' habit of sitting in an armchair with his hair-trigger and a hundred boxer cartridges and proceeding "to adorn the opposite wall with a patriotic V. R. done in bullet-pocks." He feels strongly that neither the room nor its atmosphere is in any way improved by it. One wonders also what the landlady thought. On the subject of landladies, Mrs Turner brings in the tray in 'A Scandal in Bohemia' and Holmes turns hungrily on "the simple fare our landlady has *provided*" [my italics]. Is Mrs. Turner a servant or a friend? She is not mentioned again, except in the manuscript of 'The Empty House', and only a passing reference is made to Mrs. Hudson when she brings in Mary Morstan's card on a brass salver in *The Sign of Four*. Mrs Hudson will appear again in 'The Speckled Band'. Is she a relative of Mrs Turner, who has retired and gone to live in the country? The text can be read in several ways. But it's difficult to tell what Mrs. Turner's position really is, or how she fits into the household. But something we do know is that Mrs Hudson was paid an excellent rent and gradually became very fond of Holmes, giving him material help in 'The Empty House' once Watson decided to publish it, and coming to the latter in great distress when she thinks her lodger is dying. It can only be hoped that, because of these two factors, she was able to put up with the pocks.

The Doctor can sometimes be found "nodding over a novel" after a hard day's work, and in 'The Five Orange Pips' is "deep in one of Clark Russell's fine sea stories." Was this *The Sea Queen* written and reviewed in 1884, two or three years before Watson decided to try his hand at writing a detective story? There were other novels of a similar nature written by Russell (1844-1911), an American ex-sailor turned journalist. These include *The Wreck of the Grosvenor* in 1875 and *Marooned* in 1892. The implication is that the Doctor had already read at least one tale of Russell's before mentioning another.

We discover during a walk he takes with Holmes and Toby the dog in *The Sign of Four* that Watson is familiar with the writings of the German novelist Johann Paul Friedrich Richter (1763-1825), coming to him by working back through Carlyle. This is a cryptic remark which needs some explanation. Holmes is holding forth about the smallness of man when pitted against the elemental forces of nature and says that, according to Richter, it is only man's appreciation of this smallness which reveals his true greatness. Coming to Richter through Carlyle, however, "is like following the brook to the parent lake." One wonders how he knows. In *A Study in Scarlet*, when Watson quotes something from Carlyle, Holmes asks who the man is: but later quotes *Frederick the Great* on his own account.

Richter wrote comically about eccentrics and in Carlyle's book, *Sartor Resartus,* is credited with making the hero Teufelsdröckh ['Devil's dung'] laugh uproariously with his whole body for the first and probably the last time in his life: and "no man who has once heartily and wholly laughed can be altogether irreclaimably bad." Although

Watson sometimes seems to lack a sense of humour, his fondness for Carlyle reveals that he does occasionally smile – even if Sherlock's denial of any knowledge of the man may have been a leg pull which he repeats dead pan in the first weeks of their acquaintance.

Although Holmes often plays the role of doctor, usually (but not always) seeming to consult Watson when he already knows the answer, the latter keeps up with the latest developments in medicine, buys progressively more prestigious practices and says he has cases of "great gravity" which prevent him from being entirely at Sherlock's beck and call. He is aware that railway accidents can sometimes be extremely serious and is fully prepared when a railway employee knocks on the door of his consulting room – even if, in this instance, the horrific injury is the result of something else. In *The Sign of Four* Watson says he "hurried away to my desk and plunged furiously into the latest treatise on pathology." He is trying to get away from "dangerous thoughts" of Mary Morstan, a woman likely to become very wealthy indeed and so out of reach as the wife of an ex-army surgeon "with a weak leg and a weaker bank account." Fortunately the Agra Treasure is lost and Watson can propose and be accepted.

He reads *The British Medical Journal,* and makes it plain to a gratified Percy Trevelyan in 'The Resident Patient' that he has read his monograph on obscure nervous lesions, something even the author's publishers say is not selling at all well. "I so seldom hear of the work that I thought it was quite dead." However, Watson admits, in *The Hound of the Baskervilles,* that his medical shelf in the Baker Street sitting room is "small." But he has an up-to-date copy of The Medical Directory, which reveals that Dr. Mortimer has contributed articles to *The Lancet* and *The*

Journal of Psychology. Watson may have an interest in psychology himself. In 'The Six Napoleons' he suggests that stealing and smashing the busts is an example of an obsessional neurosis, the *idée fixe*. He also reads the latest treatise on surgery, *and* studies the society gossip columns in the newspapers. This latter enables him to fill Holmes in on various matters connected with the aristocracy. He is an avid reader of newspapers, such as the *Telegraph* and the *Standard* both for himself and for Holmes, who often employs him as a person useful for reading aloud; and is first with the news that John Openshaw ('The Five Orange Pips') has been murdered. He also knows ('The Illustrious Client') that Sir James Damery is "a household name in society."

Holmes, who likes to keep his aces up his sleeve and puts Watson off with the seemingly inconsequential remark, "My fiddle would be the better for new strings", also has several literary ploys to forestall his friend's eager but importunate questions. Questions which, if answered there and then, might allow the reader to guess the outcome of his investigations prematurely: "And now here is my pocket Petrarch, and not another word shall I say of this case until we are on the scene of action." On another occasion he prefers to discuss George Meredith rather than the current case.

Petrarch (1304 -1374) had as his muse Laura, a woman he may never have met in the flesh, such was the rarified atmosphere of 'courtly love', but who may well have been a member of the de Noves family and possibly the wife of Count Hugues, or Hugh, de Sade, although she has never been positively identified as such. But if so, she was a fourteenth century ancestor of the Marquis de Sade. Petrarch's *canzone,* or *rime,* a collection of Italian sonnets written in her honour, was very popular in the nineteenth century and there were several translations of his poems available. Pocket editions, roughly four inches by six, of many authors who were not poets were also very popular towards the end of the nineteenth century. These were produced by, among others, Routledge's Pocket Library and Cassell's National Library. Watson doesn't tell us if Holmes was reading Petrarch in the original, but at any rate his friend doesn't throw any quotations in Italian at him.

George Meredith wrote a Sonnet Sequence called *Modern Love* at a time when such sequences were being made fashionable by the Rossettis. This Sequence, like Dante Gabriel Rossetti's *House of Life,* was largely autobiographical and tells the story of his failed first marriage. It's difficult to imagine Holmes being interested in anything concerning the tender emotions, even if Watson is something of a romantic. Sherlock felt women were untrustworthy, and that love interfered with the logical processes of detection. In spite of modern writers going against the text and saddling him with a wife, he said that he would never marry for fear it clouded his judgement. But, in showing an admiration for Meredith, he may have been thinking of his *An Essay on Comedy and the Uses of the Comic Spirit.* One of these 'Uses' was "to hold up a mirror to ourselves." This is something such a seemingly conventional man as Watson might think it unnecessary to do. But somehow one feels it would strongly appeal to his friend. All of which, however, contradicts the Doctor's statement in *A Study in Scarlet* that this friend's knowledge of literature is "nil". But maybe it developed over the years.

In 'The Empty House' Holmes poses as an old bookseller and carries about with him an odd collection of titles. Most of them, for example *British Birds, The Holy*

War and, a little more oddly, *The Origin of Tree Worship*, are innocent enough. But he also has a volume of Catullus, the Roman poet who wrote passionate and sexually explicit lines to 'Lesbia' [real name, Clodia] and knew what it was to both love and hate the object of his desire: "*odi et amo.*" One could say a bookseller collects anything that he thinks might sell. But later, when Holmes reveals he is still alive (causing poor Watson to faint "for the first and the last time in my life") and offers the now redundant books to his old colleague to fill a gap on the second shelf in his consulting room, he doesn't forget Catullus. But Watson doesn't say if he reads any of these gratuitously presented tomes.

Anyone with any aspirations to culture would perhaps put art and music as well as literature into what Sherlock, at the beginning of his acquaintance with Watson, termed his 'brain attic'. Holmes, however, will have none of it. The skilful workman "will have nothing but the tools which may help him in doing his work." Watson is deeply concerned that his fellow lodger, for example, knows nothing about the solar system. Neither is he interested in philosophy. Concerning the subjects Holmes does seem to have put in varying degrees into what he also calls his "little attic of a brain" – botany, politics, sensational literature, geology – can one assume that Watson knows enough about these subjects to be able to assess Holmes' expertise in each of them? If so, he has had a wide and solid education of which his old school (thought by some commentators to be Wellington College at Crowthorne, near Sandhurst, because of its strong military connections) and his university might justly be proud. And, since we would expect a doctor to know more about anatomy and chemistry than a detective, we shouldn't be surprised when Watson, intent on finding out as much as he can about his new acquaintance – so much so that he goes about making lists "like any parlour-maid" – feels able to pronounce the first "Accurate but unsystematic" and the second "Profound."

Inspector MacDonald ("Mr. Mac") doesn't recognise a Greuze when he sees one in Moriarty's study: "A young woman with her head on her hands, keeking at you sideways." But Holmes enlightens him on its importance by using *La Jeune Fille à l'agneau* as an example of that painter's work which he says is worth forty thousand pounds, and so quite beyond a professor's salary of seven hundred a year if Moriarty wasn't getting money from somewhere else. Obviously, in spite of what he said to Watson, to Holmes everything is of importance when it comes to defeating a 'Napoleon of Crime.'

Jean-Baptist Greuze (1725-1805), whose work became extremely popular in nineteenth century Britain through the medium of engravings, specialised in genre paintings of highly moral subjects and seems at first glance a strange choice for Moriarty. However, he has not only made a good investment but reinforced a false reputation for probity.

At some time during their life together Holmes tells the Doctor that his grandmother was the sister of the French painter Vernet. Later he will send a distant relative ('Dr. Verner') to buy Watson's Practice in order to persuade him to come back to Baker Street. The Vernets were a family of artists: Claude-Joseph (1714 -1789), Charles-Horace (1758 -1835) and Emile-Jean-Horace (1788-1863). The elder Vernet specialised in landscapes and was much admired by British visitors to France. Charles ('Carle') painted battle scenes for Napoleon, and Emile was a military artist for the Emperor before turning to animal and oriental subjects. He later became the Director of the French *Academie* and worked on the *Chambre des Deputies*. If Sherlock was born in 1854, Emile is the Vernet most likely to have been his 'great-uncle'.

Watson tells us in 'The Red-Headed League' (once again contradicting what Sherlock rather peevishly said to him in *A Study in Scarlet* about his brain attic) that Holmes was an enthusiastic musician and a very capable performer on the violin, as well as a composer of no ordinary merit. Unfortunately, he often exacerbated the Doctor's nerves when in contemplative mood by laying his instrument across his knees and drawing forth very unmusical noises. This posture seems extremely awkward, leading one to think the violin strings were being plucked pizzicato. We get the impression from Watson that the sound produced was more melancholy than one would expect from this way of playing. But perhaps it was simply monotonous. We are soon back with the sort of music the listener liked to hear: "I might have rebelled against these exasperating solos had it not been that he usually terminated them by playing in quick succession a whole series of my favourite airs as a slight compensation for the trial upon my patience." Watson later says of Holmes, "That he could play pieces, and difficult pieces, I knew well because at my request he has played me some of Mendelssohn's Lieder and other favourites."

"Sarasate plays at the St. James's Hall this afternoon. What do you think, Watson? Could your patients spare you for a few hours? I observe that there is a good deal of German music on the programme, which is more to my taste than Italian or French. It is introspective, and I want to introspect." They are "off to violin-land, where all is sweetness and delicacy, and harmony, and there are no red-headed clients to vex us with their conundrums." It may be that Watson, despite his fondness for Mendelssohn, would have preferred Italian or French music as more lively and more akin to military airs. But he goes willingly to St. James's Hall and watches Holmes sitting beside him in the stalls "gently waving his long thin fingers in time to the music." It's devoutly to be hoped that this was done unobtrusively and caught only by Watson, since such an ostentatious action is still seen by most British concert goers as not quite the thing – almost as bad as clapping between the movements of a concerto or a symphony.

However, having seen how Holmes' suggestion that the two friends attend Madame Norman Neruda's concert seriously compromises the chronology of *A Study in Scarlet*, introducing Pablo Sarasate, another brilliant violinist, into the canon also presents a problem. Sarasate performed frequently in London, making his first appearance there in 1861. When he didn't attract much attention until he returned in 1874. Three years later he played at the Crystal Palace, and was at the Birmingham Festival in 1885. Born in Pamplona in 1844, he trained at the Paris Conservatory, composed attractive music for his instrument and was the cause of others doing so.

Although his use of the violin was unusually individualistic, he was almost as popular as the even more successful German violinist, Joachim. The latter was the all-time favourite with the British public, and his visits to Britain with his 'Joachim Quartet' were amongst the most eagerly anticipated of all musical events. Since Joachim's programmes, while being very well attended, were exclusively German why did Holmes seem so enamoured of Sarasate, especially as he says he prefers German music? For example, he specifically mentions in 'The Red Circle' how fond he is of Wagner. Did Watson, that man of action, nod yet again? Probably not. Sherlock prefers thoughtful music when on a case. Once it's solved he can relax over more light-hearted stuff. Such references, if they do nothing else, help to date some of the Adventures.

Having once persuaded Watson to accompany him to a Sarasate Recital, Holmes is later ready to do the same thing when it comes to two Polish artistes, this time singers. At the conclusion of the investigation into *The Hound of the Baskervilles* he says, "And now, my dear Watson, we have had some weeks of severe work, and for one evening, I think, we may turn our thoughts into more pleasant channels. I have a box for 'Les Huguenots'. Have you heard the De Reszkes? Might I trouble you then to be ready in half an hour, and we can stop at Marcini's for a little supper on the way?" Edouard De Reszke (1853-1917) was a Polish singer very successful in Wagner roles. Immensely tall, having a powerfully dramatic sense combined with a strong stage personality, he became one of the greatest basses in operatic history. His brother Jean (1859-1925) began as a baritone and, after further study, emerged as a tenor. His musicianship and phrasing were considered impeccable and the beauty of his voice made him, like his brother as a bass, one of the greatest tenors of all time. Edouard made his debut at Covent Garden in 1880 and came to London regularly until his retirement in 1903. His stage presence, and especially his mastery of Wagner, would obviously appeal to Holmes if the detective was genuinely fond of German music. So would the elder De Reszke's ability as an actor: Watson never tires of telling his readers how good Sherlock is when it comes to playing a part.

There's little doubt Holmes admired both brothers since he talks of 'the De Reszkes'. Jean De Reszke sang at

Drury Lane in 1887 during Augustus Harris's first Grand Opera season there, and came to London nearly every year until 1901 before retiring to teach in Paris and Nice. This, of course, along with what we know of Edouard's engagements, would also help to date the Holmes/Watson investigations. The older singer, unfortunately, wasn't as adaptable as his brother. He made no headway as a teacher and retired to his estate in Poland, where he died in great poverty towards the end of the First World War. But, like Holmes and to a lesser extent the self-effacing Watson, his face and figure were instantly recognisable. At the height of his operatic career his picture appeared on cartons advertising cigarettes. This brought him even closer to the public, some of whom may never have entered an Opera House. But, in spite of his interest in different tobaccos, Holmes makes no mention of this advertising and nothing of it appears in Watson's accounts of their Adventures. Both De Reszkes, however, were obviously of sufficient interest in 221b Baker Street for their appearance (even in an opera not to everyone's taste) to make a civilised and cultured ending to a most terrifying investigation.

Chapter Nine: On Art and Acting

Having presented Watson as an old soldier, a trusty comrade, a gifted writer and an interesting if occasionally vague historian, it may be time to consider his views on some of the other aspects of a gentleman who wishes to appear cultured. Nevertheless, it's difficult to decide from the text if Holmes' question "Have you heard the De Reszkes?" received a positive or a negative response from his biographer. If he has heard the brothers and wishes to do so again then Watson will, we're sure, be ready in the stated time. If he hasn't, then we can be equally certain from his past behaviour that he will be very happy to accompany Holmes and certainly won't keep his imperious and impatient friend waiting. Perhaps the Doctor thoroughly enjoys Meyerbeer's rousing martial music. Because he hasn't Holmes' power of withdrawing for a while from a case, every investigation fully occupies his mind until it is finally solved. Now that Stapleton has been unmasked in *The Hound of the Baskervilles* will Watson look upon his evening in a box at the opera as a welcome relaxation? He won't forget the incident of course. It will be written up, and he may even have made notes during the boring bits that night. But it will no longer be a worry to him.

Near the beginning of Watson's account of the Baskerville case, the two friends decide to "drop into one of the Bond Street picture galleries" to see an exhibition of work by what Watson calls "the modern Belgian masters" and where, he tells us, Holmes was entirely absorbed for two hours. Afterwards, walking from the gallery to the Northumberland Hotel, "He [Holmes] would talk of

nothing but art, of which he had the crudest ideas…" [3]
Does this mean Sherlock knew little or nothing about the subject, or that he appreciated rough art? The *Les Vingts* group of Belgian artists included the misogynistic, obscene and satanic symbolist painter and engraver Rops, and the half-English Ensor – who specialised in paintings combining a madly carnival atmosphere with macabre intimations of death, dressing up skeletons in his studio and painting them fighting over a dead body.

The Times for July 3rd 1872 (when Conan Doyle was twenty-three) reported that 'Continental Artists' were exhibiting their paintings at the Bond Street Gallery, but Exhibitions in Brussels by 'The Twenty' between 1884 and 1893 were extremely controversial, particularly the drawings by Ensor of *The Devil leading Christ into Hell* and another showing a contemporary Christ entering the Belgian Capital carrying a Socialist banner. When, according to Ensor, He would receive the same treatment as He had in Jerusalem. Did these artists also exhibit in London at some time in the late eighteen eighties? They seem to have confined themselves to exhibiting in Brussels, with an occasional sortie to Amsterdam, although Ensor is recorded as paying short visits to Paris and London. Not having Holmes' "remarkable power of detaching his mind at will" Watson says nothing of his own reactions to the paintings (whatever they were), giving the impression that any "discussion" afterwards was somewhat one-sided, although some of the artists in the *Les Vingts* group, for example Gustave Vanaise or Frans Simon if they were on exhibition, might have appealed to him. And Holmes, that great upholder (if it suits him) of the status quo when it

---

[3] Sherlock later disproves this view by showing how much he does know on the subject

comes to crime, shows some startling interests: from injecting himself with a seven per cent solution of cocaine to studying possibly pornographic art. And it becomes clear later that, in spite of Watson's assertion, his friend at least knows enough about art to identify the painters of the family portraits at Baskerville Hall.

It is interesting to see that, although Watson's account of *The Hound of the Baskervilles* didn't find its way into *The Strand Magazine* until 1901, the investigation is quite definitely dated 1889. This is from the evidence of Dr. Mortimer's stick, which was presented to him when he left Charing Cross Hospital to get married and start practising medicine in the country: "And he left five years ago – the date [1884] is on the stick," says Sherlock. So what are we to make of Holmes' request to his colleague that, if the latter is going out, "It would be as well if you could make it convenient not to return before evening"? It is at the hour of action that the old soldier is wanted. But, to echo Watson's words, for the present the detective needs to spend hours in intense mental concentration – weighing every particle of evidence and constructing alternative theories, balancing one against the other until he has made up his mind which points are essential and which immaterial. The amount of tobacco he'll need to consume while doing this (and which will make Watson cough like mad when he does come back) is the reason why Holmes asks him to arrange for a pound of the strongest shag to be sent up from Bradley's the Tobacconist's for his black clay pipe. But why, when Watson returns, does Holmes deduce at once that he has been at his club all day? In 'A Scandal in Bohemia' we know that by March 1888 the Doctor was married and had returned to civil practice. Surely it's reasonable to suppose that he may have spent the day with his wife or his patients? There is, however, more than a hint that Watson is living in Baker Street and, with such specific dating, this problem cannot be brushed aside by saying that *The Hound* is an older investigation - even if it is presented as taking place before Holmes and Moriarty supposedly went over the Reichenbach Falls. But is this kind of confusion enough to make some commentators suggest the Doctor was not married to Mary Morstan until 1889? In an article, "Railways and Roads in 'The Hound'", published in 'The Sherlock Holmes Journal', Winter 1979/Summer 1980, Bernard Davies put forward the hypothesis that the investigation into *The Hound of the Baskervilles* took place in 1900.[4] By then, of course, Watson was a widower and *had* moved back to his old lodgings in Baker Street. Which he presumably didn't leave until he married again in 1903.[5]

Sherlock is not only interested in modern art and the relatively modern songs sung by the De Reszke brothers. He is also very keen on medieval music. Watson mentions in 'The Bruce-Partington Plans' that Holmes has a new hobby: 'The Polyphonic Motets of Lassus', on which he is writing yet another of his many monographs. Something which when privately printed, says Watson, became "the last word on the subject." This tells us something about Holmes' enthusiastic helper. In spite of his liking for Mendelssohn, he doesn't know enough about music to realise all motets are polyphonic by their very nature. Has Sherlock slipped again, as he did when saying that Afghanistan is in the tropics? It's much more likely to have been his biographer who slipped this time.

Roland de Lassus was born in Mons in 1532 and died in

---

[4] I am indebted to Roger Johnson for bringing this article to my attention
[5] See 'The Blanched Soldier'

Munich in 1594. A boy soprano, he later wrote much for the voice, and his motets formed part of the high ground of renaissance music. Motets are for many voices, with or without the support of musical instruments. Singers employ different musical ideas for phrases. They do this by something known as imitation, the constant restatement of identical or near identical material. Two or more melodic lines combine, and either each voice enters the same material at different points or is given an individual piece. In both cases these interventions can be of equal or unequal value and may be loosely compared to part-singing. Watson has told us that his friend is a fine musician, and a thorough knowledge of music is needed to fully appreciate the structure of motets.

Besides literature, art and music there are other media for our heroes. Ones which again raise the question "Will the world ever tire of Holmes or weary of Watson?" Drawings, theatrical adaptations, films and television have all contributed to building up complete personalities for the two men and giving them an independent existence. So much so that, as touched on earlier, the deerstalker and pipe alone are sufficient to evoke Holmes and, by association, Watson – in the same way as it is difficult to imagine Snow White without her small companions, or Alice without the White Rabbit. Considering what can be done, and is done, to the Holmes/Watson body of work, roles are sometimes reversed; and in, for example, *Without a Clue* – a film which left one critic wondering why such a "witless spoof" was ever released –Watson becomes the one with the deductive brain. There have been junior Holmes and Watsons as well as female ones: and a very early *Sheerluck Jones*. Animation, using bloodhounds smoking pipes and wearing deerstalkers, sells every-day products, even washing powder. There's no need to spell it out. The image is enough. In a letter, written from abroad during the Great Hiatus and reproduced without Watson's permission in *The Illustrated London News*, Holmes begs the Beecham Company to send him a large box of their pills "Because in this benighted spot – although you will scarcely credit it – I cannot procure what I much need."

Watson's account of the investigation *A Study in Scarlet* was first illustrated by D. H. Friston in *Beeton's Christmas Annual for 1887*. When the story was published separately the following year the author's father, Charles Doyle, gave Holmes a beard. And, according to S. C. Roberts, Charles Kerr's illustrations for *The Sign of Four* made the Great Detective look like "a melodramatic villain and Watson like a startled archduke." When the Doctor began writing for *The Strand Magazine* it was suggested that Walter Stanley Paget, who was already well-known for his dark and savage illustrations for H. Rider Haggard's *King Solomon's Mines*, as well as Robert Louis Stevenson's *Treasure Island* and Daniel Defoe's *Robinson Crusoe*, might be the very man to do the drawings. However, the letter from the editor offering the commission was mistakenly addressed to Walter's brother, Sidney Edward Paget. Born in London in 1860, the fifth child and fourth son of the musician Martha Clarke and her husband Robert Paget, the Vestry Clerk of Clerkenwell,[6] Sidney had won several prizes during his time at The Royal Academy and The Slade School of Art. According to many commentators, he emerged as a good illustrator. His drawings, however, for the Holmes/Watson Adventures did not meet with the writer's full approval. They took liberties

---

[6] A post more or less equivalent to that of a Chief Executive of a London Borough today.

with Holmes, who some said was coming more and more to resemble Sidney's strikingly handsome brother. While it is perfectly true that in one of the illustrations for 'The Red-Headed League' a rather good-looking Holmes is listening rapturously to music, Henry Marriott Paget (another brother born in 1836 and also an illustrator) wrote in *The Oxford Dictionary of Biography* for 1912: "The assertion that the artist's brother Walter, or any other person, served as a model for the portrait of Sherlock Holmes is incorrect."

In the series of illustrations Sidney Paget produced for *The Strand Magazine* from 1891 until his premature death in 1908 the best are where the figures are seated, either in Baker Street or in a train or carriage en route for their investigations. He isn't so effective in scenes of high emotion, for example when Pycroft shakes his clenched fists in the air in 'The Stockbroker's Clerk'; or the wife in 'The Yellow Face' makes a confession to her husband that, formerly married to an African-American, she is concealing a black child. The drawings by Howard Elcock for the later tales, for example 'The Creeping Man' published in the *Strand* in 1923, present the main protagonists as more human and more modern. They are real people who, apart from the dress and perhaps Watson's moustache, we might meet every day. There is, however, in the Adventures illustrated by Paget a sharpness and an economy of line which makes them instantly recognisable. It was his drawings, allied to the text, which led Professor Roberts to say that "Visual images perfectly harmonising with the spirit and the atmosphere of the narrative, combined to impart a physical realism to No. 221b Baker Street and its famous lodgers."

Although Watson sometimes wearied of Holmes, in spite of his loyal remarks to the contrary, after the first twenty-four investigations he went on to record many others. It became more and more difficult to refuse the enormous fees offered by the publisher George Newnes, who is said to have sold at least twenty-thousand extra copies of *The Strand* every time one of Watson's accounts appeared. After 1908, however, Watson had to be content with a wide variety of illustrators. These included Howard Elcock, A. Gilbert and Frank Wiles – who produced more than thirty drawings for *The Valley of Fear*. Walter Paget finally got his chance when he was asked by the editor Greenhaugh Smith to illustrate the distressing story of 'The Dying Detective'.

But it was Sidney's drawings which defined Holmes and Watson for the masses and made the two men so familiar to the magazine's readers, as well as to us. Later drawings for the stories written after his death didn't have the same impact. More lively perhaps, and less mannered, they are somehow too diffuse and lacking the tautness which Paget employed, the artists' names for the most part forgotten. These later drawings present the familiar characters differently, especially after the *Strand* changed its style. There's a touch of 'the penny dreadful' about them. They belong more properly to the pulp magazines so disliked by Joe Bell.

Theatrical adaptations of the investigations appeared quite early on, including one by Sir Arthur Conan Doyle himself based on Watson's account of the Indian swamp adder belonging to the murderous Doctor Roylott. *The Speckled Band* opened first at the Adelphi Theatre before transferring to The Globe, and showed Holmes with a waiting room full of clients, including the blackmailer Charles Augustus Milverton and Professor Moriarty. Billy the page-boy is also there behaving insufferably, smashing

Holmes' cocaine bottle when he most needs it and patronising Watson for all he's worth: "The Pope's bothering us again, wants us to go to Rome over the Cameo robbery. We are very overworked."

In the Adelphi production Lynn Harding played the dangerous Doctor Roylott (changed for some mysterious reason to Rylott for this production) and H. A. Saintsbury played Holmes, with Claude King as Watson. A real snake was later replaced by a fake, so cleverly jointed and held together by threads invisible to the audience that it could move with dreadful realism even away from the bell-rope. When Rylott utters a dreadful scream, showing he has got his just deserts, the weird reed music being played more and more loudly by his Indian servant suddenly stops dead. A beam of yellow light floods the stage and reveals the snake, a 'speckled band', wrapped round the unfortunate man's head. Uncoiling slowly, the reptile slithers down to the floor where, in a reversal of roles, Watson beats it repeatedly with his stick. Turning to Holmes for the final curtain he says, "The brute is dead." To which Holmes replies, with a glance at Rylott, "So is the other."

Sherlock Holmes, another play by Doyle written in 1898, had a chequered history. It was first sent it to the actor manager Sir Herbert Beerbohm Tree. But, when certain changes were proposed, the script was recovered and sent by Doyle's Literary Agent to the American producer Charles Frohman. Frohman showed it to William Gillette who re-wrote the play, basing his version mainly on 'A Scandal in Bohemia' and 'The Final Problem', and then lost it in a hotel fire when he was playing at a theatre in San Francisco. He almost immediately re-wrote the play as he had first conceived it, after asking the original author if he could 'marry' Holmes. The answer was "Marry him or murder him." It was all the same to Doyle. In spite of such liberties with the canon, however, Gillette's stage presence and his restrained style of acting guaranteed the success of his play (which premiered on Broadway in November, 1899 and at the Shakespeare Theatre, Liverpool, in September 1901) for over thirty years. Sherlock Holmes is seen lounging in Baker Street dressed in a paisley style dressing gown, wearing embroidered slippers and smoking a bent briar pipe, a departure from Sidney Paget's illustrations in *The Strand Magazine* which show a straight briar but chosen as being easy to handle and not obscuring the actor's mouth. The lean profile, a pipe and the dressing gown were part of Holmes' persona as soon as he became popular in *The Strand Magazine.* Watson simply says Holmes smoked an "old briar-root pipe", or a long cherrywood pipe when he was in an argumentative mood. However, the bent briar was personally approved by the author for the William Gillette play when it premiered in London in 1901 and used by Doyle in his own play staged nine years later.

When travelling, for example to the Boscombe Valley, Holmes wore 'a close-fitting cloth cap'. This became an 'earflapped travelling cap' in 'Silver Blaze'. But in both instances Sidney Paget has drawn a deerstalker. The artist himself had one, which his daughter Winifred Paget said he "found suitable for tramping about the countryside." It survived him for many years before becoming so moth-infested that his wife had to throw it in the dustbin. After *The Return of Sherlock Holmes* in 1903 Sidney included deerstalkers in at least five of his six his illustrations, although nothing resembling such headgear is mentioned in the text. But, thanks to him and William Gillette, both the deerstalker and the curved pipe would be forever associated with the detective's persona. So much so that, as Bill Blackbeard says in his introduction to a collection of articles by various authors for the book *Sherlock Holmes in America*, "The origins of this Trinity, its acceptance by now as the graphic quintessence of Holmes, is universal. Don a deerstalker, clench a calabash [sic] in your teeth, display a magnifying glass in one hand and take a stroll down Piccadilly or Main Street [and hear] "Sherlock Holmes! He thinks he's Sherlock Holmes!"'

After the triumph in America and the premiere in Liverpool Gillette brought his play to London, where it opened on September 9th 1901 at the Lyceum. Billed as 'A hitherto unpublished episode in the career of the Great Detective and showing his connection with *The Strange Case of Miss Faulkner'*, the production nevertheless contained echoes of several of Watson's reports already published. And in 1905 Gillette wrote, and starred in, a comic sequel: *The Painful Predicament of Sherlock Holmes.*

Taking an echo, or in this case a line, from the canon as inspiration for a Holmes/Watson effort of one's own continues right up to the present day. A series of four plays, *The Further Adventures of Sherlock Holmes* with Andrew Sachs as a fine Watson, were each developed from single sentences taken out of the Doctor's accounts of his erratic friend's various investigations and broadcast on BBC Radio Four in 2002. There have been three more series since then, and of course the recent Guy Richie film and the new television series on Holmes and Watson produced by the BBC have attracted a great deal of sometimes frenzied attention.

C. A. Lejeune, Film Critic for the *Observer*, wrote the script for a high-profile, six-part series about Holmes and

Watson which was aired by the BBC between October 20th and the beginning of December 1951, but more recent adaptations for television have not always been kind to Watson. They sometimes portray him, for example in the 1968 productions of *A Study in Scarlet* and *The Sign of Four*, as middle-aged and running to fat in spite of a text which describes him as being in his late twenties or early thirties at that time and exceptionally thin. He is also, as noted earlier, shown as remarkably ugly. This again goes against the text. The Doctor is occasionally made to behave in a silly way too. While a world-weary detective in the shape of Jeremy Brett, pointedly ignores the King of Bohemia's outstretched hand on taking leave of him, Watson is made to click his heels together and bow. Perhaps a piece of sarcasm which doesn't quite come off? Or a sly echo of pseudo-Prussian militarism? Holmes' rudeness to the King has possibly caught a normally courteous Watson on the hop. Protocol demands that he bow (although the heel-clicking of David Burke is, in my opinion, a bit much) before rushing off after Sherlock in the Granada TV 1984 production of 'A Scandal in Bohemia'.

Besides appearing in various plays and on television, Holmes and Watson also have a long history on the big screen. For five years from 1903 American one-reelers were being churned out for home consumption. Over the next five years one-reelers were made in Denmark, France and Germany, the latter also producing a full-length version of *The Hound of the Baskervilles* in 1917. Full-length versions of *The Sign of Four* and *A Study in Scarlet* were made in Britain before a series of short films starring Eille Norwood as Holmes appeared in 1921, as did *The Hound of the Baskervilles.* William Gillette himself had starred as Holmes in a film of his own play in 1916. But no copies are known to exist and stills from the film show a man so stiff with make-up and so undemonstrative that little idea can be given of his 'live' performances.

In 1929 came the first 'talkie'. This was *The Return of Sherlock Holmes* with Clive Brook and H. Reeves-Smith. The gaunt British actor Arthur Wontner, who the film critic Halliwell calls "a perfect" and "a splendid if elderly" Holmes, played the character in several films. The first was in 1931, when he was fifty-six. That same year the Canadian actor Raymond Massey appeared with Athole Stewart in *The Speckled Band*. And in 1932 Clive Brook was Holmes again to Reginald Owen's Watson in a film named after the main character. Owen played Holmes the following year, and had such a long and varied career that he appeared in *Bedknobs and Broomsticks* in 1971, a year before his death at the age of eighty-five. It seemed that a film about Holmes and Watson was being made, either in Britain or America, every year during the thirties; and in 1939 Basil Rathbone, according to Halliwell "The one and only Sherlock Holmes", and Nigel Bruce, "The screen's most memorable Watson," played together so successfully in *The Hound of the Baskervilles* that *The Adventures of Sherlock Holmes* was hurriedly put together for them. Supposedly based on Gillette's play, the film bore little resemblance to it and was followed by twelve modernised tales from the canon in which the original stories were almost unrecognisable.

These twelve films, however, successfully reproduced the atmosphere and dialogue of the original, beginning with *Sherlock Holmes and the Voice of Terror*. Made in wartime, this leaned heavily enough towards the war service of Sherlock Holmes for a slice of the original dialogue to be included at the finish. 'Von Bork' has been unmasked as a

Quisling in the war cabinet. As he is taken away Holmes says to Watson, "Stand with me here upon the terrace, for it may be the last quiet talk that we shall ever have. There is an east wind coming. Such a wind as never blew on England yet. It will be cold and bitter and a good many of us may wither before its blast. But it's God's own wind none the less, and a cleaner, better land will lie in the sunshine when the storm has cleared." Good, patriotic stuff designed, like the original published in 1917, to put heart into a war-torn Britain. Watson, the ever-willing helper, stands ready to drive them back to London after a last glance at the deceptively quiet moonlit sea. His work again gets a screen credit in 'Sherlock Holmes and the Secret Weapon'. The weapon this time is a bombsight stolen by Nazi agents and the film is based loosely on 'The Dancing Men'.

1943 sees Holmes and Watson in Washington once more foiling Nazi spies by stealing a microfilmed document concealed in a match folder. In *Sherlock Holmes Faces Death* (along with Doctor Watson) a series of weird murders takes place in a convalescent home for retired officers. Nevertheless, Halliwell says that "This is one of the better entries in this rather likeable modernised series; fairly close to the original story ['The Musgrave Ritual'] except that the events don't make a lot of sense." But then the story as told to Watson by Holmes in *The Strand Magazine* didn't make much sense either. It's not likely that whole generations of Musgraves would have to wait for Sherlock to solve a simple riddle – which in any case has already been worked out before Sherlock's arrival on the scene by the family butler. But as we are told that the man is an ex-teacher "able to speak several languages and play every musical instrument" this is what presumably made him a cut above the common run of servants. As Holmes says, "Your butler appears to me to have been a very clever man, and to have had a clearer insight than ten generations of his masters."

Even more mysteriously, Brunton has been in the Musgrave's service for so many years he could have found the treasure at any time once he'd solved the puzzle. One feels he wouldn't have had to wait for the help of a gullible female servant either. And when it comes to Holmes discovering the treasure's whereabouts no allowances are made either for the considerable growth of a tree over hundreds of years, the change in the calendar in the eighteenth century and the fractional change over the same period of the sun's position relative to the earth.

In *The Spider Woman* Holmes and Watson were up against a 'female Moriarty' in a film that used a variety of suspenseful episodes borrowed from a number of Watson originals. A 'sequel' to this film had no connection with the famous pair except that the same actress (Gale Sondergaad) figured in both movies, along with Rondo Hatton. He was the victim of a real-life disease which caused the bones of his face and hands to grow out of all proportion to the rest of his frame, who took the part of a 'monster'. He was a monster again in *The Pearl of Death.* This film according to Halliwell, who gave it two 'stars', had Holmes and Watson "in sparkling form" and was "certainly among the best of this series." It was based on 'The Six Napoleons', with the addition of a horror figure known as the Creeper. The female interest was supplied by a relatively minor British actress called Evelyn Ankers who had appeared in the first of the modernised Holmes/Watson sagas, *Sherlock Holmes and the Voice of Terror.* When she played the former mistress of a German agent who shot her when she betrayed him to Holmes.

It is in *Pursuit to Algiers* that we come into contact with a Watson displaying some of the characteristics we recognise in the original investigations. Easily beguiled by a luxury liner's beautiful pianist, he is perfectly happy – if a trifle bashful – to stand over her at the piano singing 'scotch airs' while all kinds of mayhem mount up around him. His fierce patriotism also causes him to make a flag out of paper when he sees Britain is not represented on board the foreign ship. Another familiar trait, his fierce loyalty to Holmes, is shown in several films. Watson insists on accompanying the detective whatever the danger, whether forbidden to do so by Sherlock or anyone else. "Of course I'll go," he asserts with dogged determination and a show of baffled surprise. "I always do." Unfortunately Nigel Bruce's portrayal of him as an amiable buffer, although it injects more humour into the investigations than the original Watson may have been intended to have, makes one wonder if he really will be all that effectual in a fight. Awfully brave, of course. Immensely willing, but…

Compensating on film for the fact that, although Watson was writing at and after the Whitechapel murders he made no mention of them, the famous pair are sometimes involved with Jack the Ripper. On one memorable occasion Sherlock, in drag, is accosted by Jack and only rescued from a gruesome death by Watson's jumping from the height of an eight-foot wall and landing on the would-be killer. In 1965 the actors John Neville and Donald Houston again involved the two men with the Ripper in *A Study in Terror,* followed in 1978 by another film in which Christopher Plummer featured as Holmes. *The Private Life of Sherlock Holmes,* directed by Billy Wilder, and starring Robert Stephens as Holmes and Colin Blakely as Watson, presents Holmes as romantically involved with a woman. This is in spite of Watson's baffled efforts in the *Strand* to interest him in Miss Violet Hunter of 'The Copper Beeches'. He is forced to present his austere friend as completely unaffected by love, once looking at a female client's bruised wrist "with the detachment of a scientist inspecting a specimen." And, although Irene Adler is usually presented as the favourite when it comes to choosing the women in Holmes' life, Watson makes it quite clear that here there was no romantic attachment. She is '*the* woman' only because she got the better of Holmes.

But there *is* another woman, one Watson (and others) largely ignore. "She listened to a short account [of the supposed murderers of her fiancé] from my companion, with a composed concentration which showed me she possessed strong character as well as great beauty. Maud Bellamy will always remain in my memory as a most complete and remarkable woman," says Sherlock in 'The Lion's Mane', an investigation he writes up himself. He has rather lost touch with Watson since his retirement, seeing him only for the occasional weekend visit. Has the Doctor been wrong all along by presenting his friend as romantically uninterested in women?

The basis of Wilder's film is a secret manuscript of Watson's. One wonders where from since, according to June Thomson's *The Secret Journals of Sherlock Holmes* (said to be compiled by a descendent of the earlier Watson) the tin box of his army days was removed to Lombard's Bank – which received a direct hit during World War II. The Doctor has obviously been remarkably careless in leaving so many of his manuscripts in all kinds of places to be suddenly discovered years later.

But having, like all authors, a natural reluctance to

destroy a good tale, this particular manuscript is said to have resulted in a scoop for the film industry. According to The National Film Theatre in 1974, the film made from it was "Affectionately conceived and flawlessly executed." Ten years later *Time Out* called it, somewhat oddly, "Wilder's least embittered film, and by far his most moving", while Halliwell termed it "A very civilised and pleasing entertainment."

Half-a-dozen television films were made in Russia once the two friends got past the censor. Vasily Litvanov was "the best Holmes ever" according to the Soviet cinemagoer. His Watson was the excellent Vitaly Solomin, and in the best socialist tradition the two men "helped people and didn't want anything in return." Which, according to a BBC programme aired in early April 2007, the ageing Litvanov felt would be a good formula for today.

Watson is nowhere to be seen outside The Sherlock Holmes Museum at '221b Baker Street, London, NW1 6XE'. But Holmes is there, complete with the deerstalker and hanging pipe, made so memorable in the portrayal of him by Gillette. A burly actor, somewhat unconvincingly dressed as a policeman, guards the house: and inside the building the first-floor sitting room has been re-created as it would have been over a hundred years ago, complete with clock, candle stick and armchairs as well as portraits and other artefacts. Very much part of Britain's literary heritage, "Visitors flock to Baker Street to see how we are perpetuating this great legend", according to the Museum's publicity material. Over two million have done so since the Museum opened, and there is no reason to suppose there will ever be a falling off of interest. Having been portrayed on stage, in film, on television and on radio, in comics ('The Hound of the Beanovilles') magazines and advertisements, there is no reason why Holmes and Watson shouldn't also be life-sized models in wax – or any other suitable material. Nor is there any reason why they shouldn't be displayed as a popular attraction for the benefit of the tourist trade. It all adds grist to the Watson mill, making every bit of his disinterested devotion and effort worthwhile – and his literary labours more famous than ever.

Chapter Ten: On Being a Prompt and Ready Traveller

As well as a faithful recorder of so many of the cases he shared with Holmes, and a willing companion when it came to visiting art galleries and concert halls, Watson is always ready (in spite of a wife and all those patients) to go anywhere with him that the Detective demands – and at the drop of a hat.

"Come at once if convenient – if not convenient come all the same," writes Sherlock. And in a somewhat less imperious telegram, which nevertheless assumes Watson's compliance, "Have you a couple of days to spare? Have just been wired for from the West of England in connection with Boscombe Valley tragedy. Shall be glad if you will come with me. Air and scenery perfect. Leave Paddington by the 11.15."

Once again the game's afoot. The old service revolver will be at the ready, and Watson will abandon everything airily assuming that Anstruther and Jackson, or some other locum, will automatically take over what, when it suits him, the Doctor describes (in 'The Red-Headed League) as "never very absorbing." Standing outside his house, complete with a hastily packed valise, one blast of the whistle carried in every gentleman's waistcoat pocket will bring him a four-wheeler, and two blasts a hansom cab. This morning he's off to Hereford. But, looking at a map of the British Isles and marking the places where his narratives are set, there are large tracts of land on which he apparently never set foot, at least in his role of faithful chronicler; with clusters where a great deal of the crime-solving in which he was involved with Holmes seems to have occurred.

London of course takes pride of place, together with the

City's suburbs. *A Study in Scarlet* revolves round Brixton. In *The Sign of Four* Miss Mary Morstan goes to the Lyceum Theatre in an attempt to solve the mystery of the pearls that come to her at periodic intervals, and most of the action in 'A Scandal in Bohemia' takes place in the area of London known as St. John's Wood. But, apart from the Metropolis, Watson's choice of which investigations to publicise seems to depend not only on the best way to exhibit his friend's "extraordinary talents" but also on certain well tried locations. 'The Five Orange Pips' is set in Sussex, as are an unlikely tale about a Vampire, and the case of 'Black Peter'. 'The Engineer's Thumb', although it begins at Watson's surgery in Paddington in the summer of 1889 – "not long after my marriage", another reason for saying Watson 'tied the knot' well after the end of the investigation into *The Sign of Four* – moves to Berkshire: and Mr. Sandeford of Reading is paid ten pounds for a bust worth fifteen shillings. Which, as soon as he leaves Baker Street, is smashed to pieces to reveal the Borgia Pearl in the mysterious affair of 'The Six Napoleons'. Helen Stoner, if she escapes from her murderous stepfather the last of the Roylotts of Stoke Moran, will marry Percy Armitage of Reading. Roylott's estate is "On the western border of Surrey." It once extended north into Berkshire and west into Hampshire, but now consists only of a few acres of ground and an old house. Watson, however, is normally very cagey when it comes to writing up reports, and at such times his accounts are unfortunately truncated and/or disguised in some way. He has to suppress certain cases altogether on occasions because of a strict embargo from Holmes. He throws titles at us without any details at all, usually to enhance his friend's reputation or because his notes are so "chaotic" he can't produce "a coherent narrative." There are some cases too of course that the world is not yet ready for.

But favourite place names do keep recurring: Surrey, the scene for 'The Solitary Cyclist' and 'The Reigate Squire', as well as 'The Speckled Band'. Kent, the venue for 'The Abbey Grange' and 'The Golden Pince-Nez'. Investigations take place in Norfolk, Hampshire, unusually in Birmingham and famously in Devon. At one point during the investigation into Neville St. Clair, alias the street beggar Hugh Boone, Holmes remarks to Watson, "We are on the outskirts of Lee [and] have touched on three English counties during our short drive, starting in Middlesex, passing over an angle of Surrey, and ending in Kent." In the early spring of 1897 the two friends find themselves in a small cottage near Poldhu Bay "at the further extremity of the Cornish peninsula." Holmes has been ordered there for his health. But very soon the extremely dangerous case of 'The Devil's Foot' intervenes before he can return to Baker Street and continue his study of "Those Chaldean roots which are surely to be traced in the Cornish branch of the great Celtic speech."

It is not necessary for an author to actually visit the places he writes about, although Watson records that he did spend that holiday in Cornwall with Holmes. Sitting in Baker Street with a pin and a good Gazetteer would have done just as well. This is especially so if Watson needed to mask for diplomatic reasons where the investigations took place. But the Doctor may have preferred to set his stories in venues he knew intimately. Or at least to borrow the names of places he was familiar with. This rings true, in spite of there being very little outside description in most of the investigations.

But more importantly there is some circumstantial

evidence Watson may have been in Holderness in the 1880s. He calls one of Holmes' clients the 'Duke of Holdernesse', whose heir has been kidnapped from The Priory School. His Grace is also 'Baron Beverley' and 'Earl of Carston', as Holmes discovers when he shoots out a long, thin arm to consult an 'encyclopaedia of reference'. But, although the Duke has a home in Wales, his main residence is in 'Hallamshire' which is an area near Sheffield, more properly called The Midlands, and not in that eponymous spit of land in East Yorkshire.

The Principal of the Priory School, Dr. Thorneycroft Huxtable, travels up "from Mackleton" to consult Holmes. But where exactly is Mackleton? It's not long before the reader is given what seems to be a definite clue. One of the few occasions when Sherlock appeals directly to his companion's expertise as a doctor is when Thorneycroft Huxtable suddenly slides to the floor in a dead faint. The Detective asks, "What is it, Watson?" The reply is: "Absolute exhaustion – possibly mere hunger and fatigue." Watson has his finger on the man's "thready pulse, where the stream of life trickled thin and small." At the same time Holmes draws "A Return ticket from Mackleton in the North of England" from the watch-pocket of the unconscious Principal's jacket and says, "It is not twelve o'clock yet. He has certainly been an early starter."

Thorneycroft Huxtable, if he arrived in Baker Street in late morning, surely travelled on a 'milk train'. This would make him a very early starter indeed. The 7 a.m. train from York to London was scheduled to arrive at 11.15 am. If the Head of "Without exception, the best and most select preparatory school in England" travelled from Hull, he would have to be at the station by 6.50 a.m., changing at Doncaster and arriving in London at 11.12 a.m. By the time he reached Baker Street it might be "not twelve o'clock yet." At some point the beleaguered man says "I think, Mr Holmes, it is time we were leaving for Euston." This would be a very roundabout way indeed from the north, necessitating an even earlier rising, even though we're told Mackleton Station isn't far from Doctor Huxtable's Establishment. By 1901 the London and North Western Line had lost its monopoly. It was quicker to come from York or Hull to King's Cross by the Great Northern.

However, if the Priory School is in Hallamshire and ten miles away from Holdernesse Hall, which is the Duke's country seat, what exactly is Watson up to? Hallamshire is an ancient Lordship associated more with Derbyshire and the Peak District than either Hull or York. The Duke has been "Lord Lieutenant of Hallamshire since 1900." He owns extensive mineral rights in Lancashire and Wales. While it is true that many ducal titles are divorced from their geographical area, is there any point in listing these titles and honours? There is nothing in the story to connect the kidnapping of Lord Saltire (named, possibly, for Saltaire in the West Riding) with 'Carston' or Beverley. 'Mackleton' seems to be firmly placed in an area nearer to Chesterfield, still an awkward journey to London for Thorneycroft Huxtable. Holmes and Watson see the two sidelights of a trap and hear the rattle of horse's hooves as it wheels out into the road and goes "at a furious pace in the direction of Chesterfield". Mention of the 'moors' and the 'Peak' don't help as these terms could apply to Derbyshire as well as Yorkshire, in spite of the frequent references to the "North of England." The Duke's Offices of State include being "Lord of the Admiralty." Watson has really gone to town with more extraneous information about a client than ever before. So is there a hidden agenda here?

By telling us Holmes has hooked such a very big fish he may be seeking to justify the precise pocketing of a £6000 cheque, once the case is concluded, by a man who often says he sees his fee as subordinate to the interest of an investigation: "My friend rubbed his thin hands together with an appearance of avidity which was a surprise to me, who knew his frugal tastes, folded up his cheque and placed it carefully in his note-book. 'I am a poor man,' said he, as he patted it affectionately and thrust it into the depths of his inner pocket."

Has Holmes suddenly developed socialistic tendencies? Has he a contempt for the Duke as a man? One who, to avoid scandal, has imperilled his marriage by keeping an illegitimate son close by him while allowing a much younger legitimate one to remain in the hands of a murderous ruffian? Watson is usually somewhat over-awed in the company of the Aristocracy. Such subtleties could have been lost on him.

There is no doubt about the day when the heir to the Duke of Holdernesse vanishes, however. "He was last seen on the night of May 13th – that is, the date of last Monday [and] his absence was discovered at seven o'clock on Tuesday morning." The Duke married in 1888 and the missing Lord Saltire is ten years old. The only relevant year when May 13th fell on a Monday was 1901, which is spot on.

Watson's weakness about train routes and times is echoed in some other Adventures, where he uses both to jazz up his accounts. The journeys themselves add little to the actual investigations, apart from in 'The Bruce-Partington Plans'. Here an understanding of the railway is crucial. But, as with the hansom cabs and the four wheelers which the pair use in London, trains add pace and excitement to the reports – even if Watson's descriptions vary in attention to detail and are not always accurate. They also give Holmes a chance to explain the facts of a case before arriving at the scene of a crime. Sidney Paget can vary his illustrations, showing Holmes leaning forward in what the text describes as "his ear flapped travelling cap", and ticking off on his fingers various points he wants to get over to his faithful scribe and companion. The Great Western Railway mainline was one of Watson's favourites, and is given several interesting treatments. The G.W.R. was well known for its speed and comfort, and despite the potential disruption caused by the conversion from broad gauge to standard gauge between 1870 and 1892, it maintained this reputation at the time of the Doctor's accounts. In *The Hound of the Baskervilles* Holmes and Watson take the 10.30 Saturday train from Paddington to the West of England, which Watson describes as "A journey swift and pleasant –a change of scenery to a richer if damper climate." He is impressed by his first sight of the desolation of Dartmoor, as is Holmes, and shortly afterwards the train pulls up at "a small wayside station." There is no mention of a change of train or of any intermediate stations, and the implication is that they are near to 'Princetown' [Dartmoor] Prison. Watson has used the old name for the prison, which is also the name of the rather large village in which the prison is arguably situated. It would seem that the pair took a through train for Plymouth or Penzance and left their compartment at Plympton. From there they would have a memorable drive across the moor to the prison, and presumably go back to the same station later to meet Lestrade and hear the London train come "roaring in."

We know from Holmes' telegram to Watson that 'The Boscombe Valley Mystery' involved another journey from Paddington on the Great Western. The date is between

1889 and 1894, after the Doctor has gone into partnership with Anstruther. The train is the 11.15 to Gloucester and thence to Ross-on-Wye. Watson doesn't mention a change of train, but one was probably necessary. If not, the carriage he shared with Holmes could be uncoupled from the Express and attached to a local train. Or, perhaps with another carriage or two added, *become* the local train. A lunch stop is to be made at Swindon during the journey. This was unavoidable before 1895 as the G.W.R. had a contract with a catering firm which obliged it to stop every one of its trains in Swindon for at least twenty minutes. Such an arrangement was not uncommon. Charles Dickens wrote in *The Uncommercial Traveller*: "You are going off by railway, from any Terminus. You have twenty minutes for dinner before you go." To him, the food was uneatable. But after 1895 the G.W.R. bought out the catering firm for a vast sum of money and could in future plan where and when, and for how long, its trains stopped.

Watson tells us that "It was nearly four o'clock when we at last, after passing through the beautiful Stroud Valley and over the broad, gleaming Severn, found ourselves at the pretty little country town of Ross." This sounds like a real observation. Conan Doyle travelled the Stroud valley route in 1885, crossing the Severn just before Gloucester on his way to Monmouth, a town nine miles from Ross. The purpose of his journey, taken with his future mother-in-law, was to draw up a marriage settlement prior to his wedding with his first wife, Louise Hawkins. Lestrade, who has met Holmes and Watson at the station in Ross, takes the pair to 'The Hereford Arms'. But Holmes is reluctant to travel to Boscombe Valley and the murder scene that evening. He prefers to inspect it the following day. Instead he goes with the Inspector to Hereford Gaol for an interview with the younger McCarthy, a prime suspect in 'The Boscombe Valley Mystery.' Watson, after seeing their train off, is left alone to amuse himself in Ross, and says that he lay upon the sofa and tried to interest himself in a yellow-backed novel. "The puny plot of the story was so thin, however, when compared with the deep mystery through which we were groping, and I found my attention wander so continually from the fiction to the fact, that I at last flung it across the room."

In 1848 W.H. Smith secured the concession to sell novels and newspapers at railway bookstalls. Ten years later he began issuing one-volume books in bright yellow covers. These 'yellow backs' were followed in due course by cheap 'shilling' novels. Such books were either reprints of existing stories or ones specially written for the bookstall customer, who could buy them to read on the train. Routledge's Railway Library, which followed Smith's lead, was enormously successful in this respect. But, according to Q.D. Leavis, neither it, nor the yellow backs offered the sort of reading which required much exertion.

The question is, how did Watson acquire such a book? Was it on Paddington Station, and did he dip into it while Holmes read newspapers, made notes and meditated? Did he start reading it when Sherlock fished out his pocket Petrarch twenty minutes from Swindon and refused to say another word about the McCarthys? Did he buy the book at Swindon? Or at Ross when, after seeing Holmes and Lestrade off at the station, he would be by himself all evening with nothing to do? It's quite likely that, in such a quiet spot as Ross then was, the station bookstall there was already closed and Watson found his yellow-back in the sitting room of his hotel, where it had been left by an earlier traveller.

There is more geographical detail than is usual with Watson in the Boscombe Valley investigation. Two of the protagonists meet by Boscombe Pool. This is surrounded by reeds and backed by woods. For the purposes of the plot a narrow swathe of grass and reeds is put between the wood and the Pool, so that the heated discussion between father and son (which apparently leads to parricide) can take place in the open. The real murderer, hiding behind a convenient tree and smoking a cigar (something which aids Sherlock in his search for clues) has to creep forward unseen to this spot to retrieve an incriminating grey cloak he has dropped near the body. A lodge, with a grand house discernible in the distance from one side of the Pool, and a farm not far distant on the other, complete the picture. A girl of fourteen, Patience Moran, the daughter of the lodge-keeper of the Boscombe Valley Estate, is picking flowers in the wood and hears the two McCarthy men having a violent quarrel at the border of the wood and close by the lake. Frightened by the strong language, and what she thought was the beginning of a fight, the girl ran home and became a valuable witness at the trial for murder of young James McCarthy.

The interesting point, for Watson as a writer searching for plausible *locales,* is that at Sellack, a small village between Ross and Hereford, there is a building that could pass for the farmhouse in question. It stands near a pool ringed by trees, into which water drains from a small declivity in the surrounding landscape. On the opposite side to this declivity is a smaller building which could pass as a lodge. A larger house stands behind this smaller building and might almost be the dwelling of the real killer, Turner, of James McCarthy's father. But it's difficult to believe in the existence of a substantial body of water at that precise spot.

Any appreciable amount coming down a valley would flow directly into the Wye. It could, however, have triggered Watson's imagination and caused him to produce such a detailed description of what happened at Boscombe Pool.

But maybe Harewood, a big estate situated about eleven miles from Ross in the direction of Hereford, is the setting for the Mystery? It has changed hands several times and been bought by men the townsfolk might see as 'outsiders'. In the train travelling from London to Ross, Holmes says, "The largest landed proprietor in that part is a Mr. John Turner, who made his money in Australia, and returned some years ago to the old country."

Local lore has it that one of Watson's more well-constructed stories, *The Hound of the Baskervilles,* was written at Clyro, a place reasonably close to Sellack. Anyone interested in his literary labours can stay at the Baskerville Arms, where the model of a wolf-like dog over the doorway is said to represent Black Vaughan. This fifteenth century baron, who seems to have been called 'black' from the colour of his hair rather than from the colour of his heart, may or may not be a fitting prototype for the horrid Sir Hugo Baskerville. But some say he behaved so badly he was changed into a dog and is said to haunt the Welsh borderlands. A mile or so out of the village on the Brecon Road is a house called Clyro Court. This was built in 1839 by Sir Thomas Baskerville and Conan Doyle is said to have stayed there at one time: which again adds some credence to the claim that the story of the 'gigantic hound' belongs here rather than in Devon. Two other characters in *The Hound of the Baskervilles* may owe their names to the area. The Mortimers were the most powerful Norman family in the Welsh Marches. Stapleton is a small hamlet between Presteigne and Kington. Be that as it may,

Clyro Court is now the Baskerville Hall Hotel. It has a sign-board facing the road and showing Sherlock wearing the famous deerstalker. But there's nothing similar for his willing helper.

Norfolk also has its tale of a spectral Dog. Black Shuck is said to haunt the coastal region. But the evidence for Devon being the source of inspiration for *The Hound* is strong. The discussions Doyle had with Fletcher Robinson, the note he appended to the tale, the fact that the Robinsons' coachman who drove the two men around as they explored the area was named Henry Baskerville and that there was a ready-made historical villain to hand (Sir Richard Cabell) all testify to this. However, it must be said that creative work is usually the result of a number of disparate 'inspirations'.

Sometime before December 1892 Holmes and Watson again head for Dartmoor from Paddington. As the train approaches Reading Holmes remarks, "We are going well. Our rate at present is fifty three and a half miles an hour..." This speed would be typical for a G.W.R. express of the period. Watson is puzzled and says, "I have not observed the quarter-mile posts." Using his superior knowledge, Holmes is able to point out that, because the telegraph posts are sixty yards apart on that particular line, "The calculation is a simple one." It would be evening before they reached Tavistock, and the start of their investigation into the disappearance of the champion race-horse, Silver Blaze. The pair later go by train to Winchester to see the disguised horse win the 'Wessex Cup', travelling back afterwards with the owner, Colonel Ross, to Victoria Station.

While it may be difficult to accept that a man couldn't recognise his own horse, even if disguised, there were a number of 'hoof-snafflers' operating in and around trainers' premises who could 'christen' [disguise] a horse so well that no one would know it. One of the most famous horses to be snaffled was a three year old from Derbyshire known as Silver Whistle, by a former magsman, or fairground cheat, called Andrew Taggart.

On the way from Portsmouth to London in 'The Naval Treaty' Holmes is cheered to see "big, isolated clumps of building rising up above the slates, like brick islands in a lead-coloured sea." He calls them "Lighthouses, my boy! Beacons of the future! Capsules with hundreds of bright little seeds in each, out of which will spring the wiser, better England of the future." The less lyrical Watson, staunchly conservative, conformist and, as far as Sherlock knows, equally the product of a privileged education, simply says, once they have been pointed out to him, "The board schools." He is puzzled by Holmes' enthusiasm at being able to come into London on lines which run high enough to allow passengers to look down on the small, crowded houses flashing by. He has noticed nothing else, and to him that view is "sordid enough." But has this piece, like his earlier rhapsodising over a rose, been put in to broaden Holmes' character and to make him appear a little less like a machine? Is his association with the not so single-minded Watson beginning to bear fruit? Perhaps. But the rose episode may have been to disguise the fact that Holmes was looking for scratches on the window sill. After all, he never told his biographer everything. Watson wrote about what he saw and heard: and immediately after the 'beacons of light' speech Sherlock asks if Phelps drinks. He is back on the case and won't deviate again until it is solved.

Watson says Holmes was profoundly thoughtful throughout the journey from Woking and hardly opened his mouth until after the train passed Clapham Junction and the board schools. Was he meditating on the prevalence of crime and thinking perhaps that education would decrease it? Watson concentrates on presenting upper class crimes such as those involving the Duke of Holdernesse, and the not quite so upper class Reigate Squire. He also writes up a fair number of political investigations involving stolen plans. The nearest he gets to a possible product of the board schools is Miss Mary Sutherland and her stepfather in 'A Case of Identity', both of whom are probably too old to have attended one.

But to return to Holmes' and Watson's travels together, and the latter's plan to evade Professor Moriarty and his henchmen in 'The Final Problem', this is an Adventure which raises several questions. Either Holmes had not thought the possibilities through fully enough, or Watson's memories are faulty. Obviously the Doctor considered some details more important than others but, in the stress of writing about his friend's supposed death, only succeeded in muddying the waters. An elaborate ploy is devised by Holmes to decoy the Doctor onto the Continental Express, and a reserved first class carriage second from the front of the train. Sherlock, who intends leaving the train somewhere along the line, is already there disguised as an Italian priest. Watson spends some time helping this personage with his luggage, and trying to impress on "my decrepit Italian friend" that he should find another carriage as quickly as possible. But then, to his "uncontrollable astonishment," the old ecclesiastic speaks to him: "My dear Watson," said a voice, "you have not even condescended to say good morning."

Earlier, carefully following Holmes' very complicated instructions, Watson leaves home at a quarter past nine in the morning and arrives at Victoria Station seven minutes before train departure time. The information given to him, that Holmes intends making a stop at Canterbury, shows that the pair travelled on the London, Chatham and Dover Railway. From Canterbury, Holmes and Watson intend to make a cross-country journey to Newhaven, letting their luggage go on to Paris as a blind. The station at Canterbury East would certainly not be able to offer any suitable train for this, and the two friends would have to cross to Canterbury West to catch a train to Ashford. From there they might, by way of Hastings or with a change at Tonbridge, eventually get themselves to Newhaven in time for the crossing to Dieppe.

But Moriarty, having shadowed Watson, arrives on the platform at Victoria just as their train shoots out of the station. It becomes vitally important to think what to do about him now the two friends know for certain that he is on their track. Watson is sanguine: "As this is an express, and as the boat runs in connection with it, I should think we have shaken him off very effectively." Holmes' sardonic reply to this is that Moriarty will hire a train and arrive in Dover in time to catch them at the boat if they follow that route. For the 'Napoleon of Crime' to hire a 'Special' was perfectly feasible. But to be able to get a 'Special' to leave at less than an hour's notice seems unlikely. The Prime Minister, Lord Salisbury, would have one ready with steam up to go to or from Hatfield at fifteen minutes notice. But a private citizen would have to wait considerably longer. Indeed, Watson has the temerity to question Holmes' statement by saying, "But it must be [too] late." The Detective disagrees. Their train stops at Canterbury for a while, and there is always at least fifteen minutes delay at the boat. Later Watson assures us that Moriarty's Special passed them "with a rattle and a roar" shortly after they left the train as planned. This sounds like a real observation – the Chatham Company's trains were notorious for rattling and roaring.

Holmes proposes that they buy carpet bags and some clothes en route and make their way at leisure to Switzerland by way of Luxembourg and Basle. It is, of course, highly likely that Watson immediately agreed to this but, obviously under tremendous strain once he returned to England without Holmes, records that they went by way of Brussels and Strasbourg.

In 1909 the *Strand* published 'The Bruce-Partington Plans', a thriller about espionage and treachery from 1895. It begins with a visit by Mycroft Holmes to Baker Street. This is so unusual that it must be something of real importance. A telegram sent to Holmes simply mentions the name 'Cadogan West.' Sherlock at first says he doesn't know the name. He admits later that he does remember it, but that he took no interest as he thought the case featureless. Is this one up to Watson, who knows a lot more about it, or a petulant put-down? The incident was in all the papers, papers which Holmes either reads avidly himself or has read to him by others. We're told he even catalogues the news sheets very carefully. But it is Watson who reminds him that Cadogan West is the name of a young man found dead on the Underground the previous Tuesday morning, and that a good many fresh facts came out at the inquest.

Arthur Cadogan West was twenty-seven years of age, unmarried, and a clerk at Woolwich Arsenal. Holmes then spots the possible link with Mycroft who, when he arrives in Baker Street, tells them that secret plans of the components of a submarine have been stolen and that some of the said plans were found in the dead man's pocket. The prevailing theory is that Cadogan West had stolen the plans and been murdered and his body thrown from a train by the spies to whom he tried to sell them. Holmes feels there is more to it than this. The body was discovered on the left-hand side of the tracks of the Metropolitan-District Underground Railway just before Aldgate Station. No ticket was found on the dead man and Aldgate is beyond London Bridge (if travelling on an eastbound train), where Cadogan West would have alighted if he had been on his way back to Woolwich. A passenger reported hearing a bump at 11.40 a.m. on the Monday, but saw nothing because of the smoky conditions. It was not possible to inspect the train as it had already been broken up and the carriages redistributed.

Holmes suggests the victim was killed elsewhere, and that the body fell off the roof of a carriage at the curve after the junction where the train emerged from a tunnel. "Consider the facts. Is it a coincidence that it is found at the very point where the train pitches and sways as it comes round on the points? Is that not the place where an object upon the roof might be expected to fall off?" The points wouldn't affect anything inside the train, and the absence of blood on the line indicated that the victim had bled elsewhere. Watson again draws attention to the absence of a ticket, and Sherlock then tries to deduce where the body might have been put on the roof.

He cheats slightly. Mycroft has given him the information (which he hasn't passed on to Watson) that a well-known foreign agent ("Mr. Hugo Oberstein") has been living near Gloucester Road. And once again, as in the Milverton investigation, Holmes inveigles Watson into making an illegal entry into the house with him. Having evaded a policeman, forced a door and gone up a curved and uncarpeted set of stairs they hear a train shudder to a halt immediately adjacent to a back window. This window has a drop of about four feet. It is obvious that a body has rested there from the blurred black surface of the sill. This is confirmed when Holmes spots a blood stain on the woodwork, much like the one he has seen earlier on the stairs. Watson writes for our benefit that they did not have long to wait. "The very next train roared from the tunnel as before, but slowed in the open, and then, with a creaking of brakes pulled up immediately beneath us." Just long enough for poor Cadogan West to be tipped out of the window onto its roof.

This would indicate a possible location at Cromwell Curve North Junction, or at Cromwell Curve East Junction between High Street Kensington and Gloucester Road, where there had also been many disputes and legal proceedings between the Metropolitan and the District Railways. Thanks to Holmes the culprits are captured and, fortunately for the sensibilities of his fiancée and *Strand* readers, the defunct Cadogan West is cleared of all blame. In addition, the secret plans are safely returned to Woolwich. Watson tells us that some six weeks later Holmes made a discreet visit to Windsor and received an emerald tie-pin "from a certain gracious lady" before returning to Baker Street and his monograph on the music of the middle ages.

But it won't be the last time he mentions his friend's involvement with Royalty.

Chapter Eleven: On Performing the One Selfish Act

In spite of being such a faithful comrade in his fight against crime, a usually careful recorder of his cases and an indefatigable travelling companion when his detective required him to be, Watson nevertheless willingly left Holmes for a wife on at least two occasions during the seventeen years they worked together. He had introduced the first Mrs Watson (née Morstan) to his readers during his involvement in *The Sign of Four* when she came to consult Holmes about some pearls which had been coming to her for some time, and a letter she received that very morning.

Considering how vague Watson is sometimes, he is unusually definite about dates here. A pearl has been posted to Miss Morstan every year since 1882 – "six years ago." And now a letter has arrived, dated July 7. According to the young woman's account (as recorded by Watson) her father, Major Morstan of the 34th Bombay Infantry, vanished on December 3rd, 1878, "nearly ten years ago." He had arrived home on leave and was staying in London at The Langham Hotel. His motherless daughter, who had been sent home from India when quite a small child but was by this time seventeen, was told to come down from her school in Edinburgh to join her father. But when she arrived he was nowhere to be found. The Captain checked his luggage into the hotel the night before, but had then gone out and not returned. Although exhaustive enquiries were made and the police informed, "From that day to this no word has ever been heard of my unfortunate father. He came home with his heart full of hope to find some peace, some comfort, and instead…"

Here a sympathetic and already smitten Watson says, "She put her hand to her throat, and a choking sob cut short the sentence." But Miss Morstan, in response to Holmes' questioning, went on to say that the first pearl arrived "to be exact, upon the fourth of May, 1882." Such precise dating, coupled with her earlier statement, would seem to indicate that the investigation into *The Sign of Four* took place in 1888. But she opens a flat box to reveal only *six* of the finest pearls that Watson has ever seen in his life, although an inscrutable Holmes reacts less openly to them. Counting 1882 as the first year a pearl arrived at Mrs. Forrester's house in Camberwell, where Mary was a governess, there should, in that case, have been seven. Since there weren't, unless the visitor had one concealed in her garter, this means Captain Morstan disappeared a year earlier than the time stated.[7] Otherwise nearly ten years ago becomes in reality nearly nine. But December 1878 would be a memorable date for Watson, at that time struggling up the Afghan passes to reach his regiment. He was obviously bowled over by Miss Morstan. Holmes had been particularly pernickety that morning, criticising the Doctor's honest efforts to put *A Study in Scarlet* before the public in an interesting way. The old soldier had drunk more wine than usual at lunch. When he came to consult his notes three years later he didn't realise he had mistaken the date, and was probably in too much of a hurry to get his copy to the editor of *Lippincott's American Magazine* to consult his wife.

---

[7] In 1932 T. S. Blakeney suggested (*Sherlock Holmes: Fact or Fiction?*) that Mary had in fact received seven pearls, but that she'd had the first one made into a brooch or a pendant, not realising there would be more. As Roger Johnson (who drew my attention to this theory) says, "It makes sense." One of my objections to it is that, as a governess, Mary would be too circumspect to draw attention to herself by showing off such a jewel. (See also my *The Sign of Fear*). And she carried the pearls to Holmes in such a snug little case!

Watson's next publication, his first for *The Strand Magazine*, says that 'A Scandal in Bohemia' took place in March 1888. In it he reveals that his marriage has drifted him away from Holmes. "My own complete happiness, and the home-centred interests which rise up around a man who first finds himself master of his own establishment, were sufficient to absorb all my attention." His has been a sudden wedding, taking place after September when the investigation into *The Sign of Four* ended, and well before March of the following year.

In 'A Case of Identity' Holmes, busy showing off his jewelled snuff-box – a present from the King of Bohemia – and the ring given him for services to the reigning family of Holland, says to Watson, "I forgot that I had not seen you for some weeks." But in 'The Five Orange Pips' Watson is back in Baker Street. His wife is "on a visit to her mother's" (even though the reader has been told in *The Sign of Four* that Miss Morstan has no relatives at all now since she has discovered her father is dead) and he is spending a few days in his "old quarters." The year is 1887, and the month September. Was Mary Morstan, like Irene Adler, married by Special Licence? And did she go off almost immediately, without stopping for a honeymoon, in the kind of dreadful weather described by Watson? "It was in the latter days of September, and the equinoctial gales had set in with exceptional violence. All day the wind had screamed and the rain had beaten against the windows..." In 'The Man with the Twisted Lip' Kate Whitney, a friend of Mrs. Watson from her school days, rushes into the house begging for help to find her missing husband. Watson tells us it is June 1889, so it seems natural to suppose he has been married for almost two years.

But in his account of the wedding ceremony between

Lord St. Simon (the 'Noble Bachelor') and the American girl Hatty Doran, he says that it took place in the month of October, "a few *weeks* [my italics] before my own marriage." Since Watson also tells us that the bridegroom was born in 1846 and is now forty-one the year would again seem to be 1887. If this is so it supports the theory that Mary Morstan did come to see Holmes for the first time that year –and with the correct number of pearls. But not that she was married as early as September. Was she a Christmas bride? A careless bridegroom has thrown everything into disarray, perhaps calling the woman his wife before she was, and forgetting that when the Orange Pips investigation took place he was still a bachelor living in Baker Street. To make matters worse, he writes that 'The Engineer's Thumb' occurred in the summer of 1889, "not long after my marriage." Of course, to such a happy and contented husband as Watson presents himself, the period between 1887 and 1889 may have seemed short, but it's not the accepted way of writing about the passage of time.

In 'The Stockbroker's Clerk' Holmes says, "I trust that Mrs Watson has entirely recovered from all the little excitements connected with our adventure of the 'Sign of Four'." It would seem to be the first time he has seen Watson since that investigation. But we know that Watson visited him in March 1888 and it's now June. Shortly after his marriage the Doctor had bought a practice in Paddington which kept him extremely busy for at least three months. But this heavy work-load must have slackened off a little (to the great relief of one or other of his locums) because Watson dropped everything and travelled to Birmingham that very day. He had already got Anstruther on a piece of string, willing to take over his surgery at a moment's notice. He says he does the same for his neighbour when that gentleman goes away, and the neighbour "is always ready to work off the debt." But considering the number of times Watson leaves his patients, and the speed with which he does so, the bargain seems somewhat one-sided. And was Mrs. Watson entirely satisfied with the hurried explanation he gave her for running off one morning, when he rushed upstairs as she was getting ready to come down to breakfast?

In 'The Crooked Man' Watson is found "One summer night, a few months after my marriage, seated by my own hearth smoking a last pipe and nodding over a novel, for my day's work had been an exhausting one." But in spite of being so tired that he is falling asleep over a book, the Doctor is more than willing to go to Aldershot the following morning with Holmes, and is in no doubt Jackson (another willing medical man) will take over his practice. Even though Holmes has deduced from the state of his boots that his friend's round that day has been long one: "I have the advantage of knowing your habits, my dear Watson. When your round is a short one you walk, and when it is a long one you use a hansom. As I perceive that your boots, although used, are by no means dirty I cannot doubt that you are at present busy enough to justify the hansom."

These two-wheeled 'gondolas of London' invented by Joseph Hansom of York competed for trade with 'safe and respectable' four-wheeled cabs, and had a slightly racy and disreputable image. Perhaps the ultra-conservative Watson would have preferred a punch carriage when engaged with his medical duties? This type of vehicle enabled a doctor to get in and out of it quickly, to write up his notes while protected from the weather, and on occasion to transport his patient to hospital. The first one was designed by an

Aberdeen coachbuilder for a country doctor, so maybe Dr. Mortimer used one down in Devon. He certainly owned a dog cart. But the punch carriages[8] never became popular in the towns and cities, and in any case Watson was probably unable to bear the cost of buying one.

To return to his locums, one wonders if Anstruther and Jackson are younger men, anxious to gain as much experience as possible in order to progress in their chosen profession. Do they feel that all this covering for Watson will be a help? If so, they're not likely to be correct, and he certainly won't be able to aid them personally. He's too busy sleuthing, and presents himself as more of a literary than a medical man. But, according to the way Watson writes about them, Anstruther and Jackson appear to be, like him when away from Holmes, simply jobbing (if unusually willing) practitioners.

"Is Mrs. Watson in?" asks Holmes in 'The Final Problem'. It's April 1891, and once again Watson's wife is "away upon a visit." Where to, and to whom, one wonders? Not to her parents or to any other relative, obviously. Was she at the house of her old employer Mrs Forester? Or staying with her friend Kate Whitney? Whatever the answer, Watson is free to travel on the Continent for a whole week with Holmes and to be in Switzerland when the detective supposedly falls, in the arms of his arch-enemy Moriarty, into the Reichenbach Falls. By Sherlock's miraculous return to London three years later in 1894, Watson's first wife would be dead and the Doctor free to sell his Kensington practice (increasing affluence causing

---

[8] It has been suggested that the name comes from the fact that the profile of the back of the carriage resembles the silhouette of Mr. Punch. (See the catalogue of the National Trust Carriage Museum at Arlington Court).

him to abandon Paddington?) and move back into Baker Street. However, 'The Veiled Lodger' is said to have taken place "early in 1896" – when Watson received a hurried note from Holmes summoning him to Baker Street. This suggests that the Doctor had not yet moved in again with Holmes or that perhaps, as seems more than likely, he had his consulting rooms elsewhere. It isn't until some years later that we hear of another marriage.

In his account of the Blanched Soldier Holmes says that he first met his client James M. Dodd in January 1903 and that Watson had left him to get married: "The only selfish action which I can recall in our association." But hadn't Watson been equally 'selfish' in marrying Miss Morstan? However, both men were young then. Holmes hadn't yet come to fully appreciate the convenience and companionship of having someone so level-headed as the Doctor always about the place. Neither did he realise how much he relied on Watson as listener, sounding board, someone to remind him to eat, to get more sleep, to read the newspapers aloud and to look up train times. Perhaps also, he had begun to like the amount of fame, and the large number of clients, that the old campaigner's literary labours must have inevitably brought him over the years.

A new wife for Watson was already forcing Holmes to write up one of his investigations for himself; something he found unexpectedly difficult especially as "it chanced that Watson had no note of it in his collection." Did the Doctor forget the case? After all, he wasn't there when it occurred. Whatever the reason for the omission, once again Holmes was left alone. Just as he had been in 1887. Only the two men were younger then and had not had time to form a close friendship. Now it would hurt more.

At the time of 'The Three Garridebs' (an investigation

which took place towards the end of June 1902) Watson was still in Baker Street. However, the Illustrious Client case has him practising as a doctor in Queen Anne Street. This crosses Harley Street, where Holmes' own Doctor Agar has his practice, and was both fashionable and prestigious. Watson has somehow or other come far since the days of his first civil practice. Was his second wife wealthy? In 'The Creeping Man' he receives a telegram from Holmes: "Come at once if convenient – if inconvenient come all the same." The doctor has become a habit with him even though, to quote Watson's own words, many of his remarks could just as appropriately be addressed to his bedstead. Wealthy or not, the faithful friend leaves his new wife, in the same way as he left Mary Morstan, and comes to Baker Street at once. To be completely ignored for half-an-hour until Holmes came out of his reverie and "greeted me back to what had once been my home."

Watson himself makes no mention at all of his second wife, who may even be his third if the rumours about the woman he is said to have met in America before his acquaintance with Holmes began are true. And if Watson married, or had an affair with, the owner of the *red* strand of hair Holmes noted in the Adelphi production of *The Speckled Band* what further proof would be needed of his experience of women in three continents? The hair Holmes pulls off the Doctor's jacket, winds carefully round his finger and inspects intently with his magnifying glass, can't belong to Mary Morstan. In *The Sign of Four* she is "a blonde young lady, small, dainty, well-gloved, and dressed in the most perfect taste." And who, according to Holmes, "might have been most useful in such work as we have been doing. She had a decided genius that way." But one wonders if the favourite candidate for the title of The Second Mrs. Watson could possibly be the right one. Would Watson, with such a taste for women of Mary's stamp, really have fallen in love with someone he describes in 'The Problem of Thor Bridge' as "a brunette, tall, with a noble figure and a commanding presence"?

A governess, like Watson's first wife, Grace Dunbar has been propositioned by her employer, the "Gold King" Neil Gibson, even though he is married. When his wife commits suicide in such a way that the governess is arrested for murder, Holmes is called in to save the girl from the gallows. This he does with resounding success, but will Gibson marry the woman he tried to make his mistress? Sherlock seems to think so saying, "Should they in future join their forces, as seems not unlikely..." But Watson has described Gibson as "iron of nerve and leathery of conscience." There is about him "a suggestion of hunger and rapacity." He has cold grey eyes, and "a remorseless face which bears the scars of many a [financial] crisis."

Miss Dunbar, on the other hand, has a sensitive face and "an innate nobility of character which would make her influence always for the good." The Doctor is struck by the "appealing, helpless expression of the hunted creature who feels the nets around it" which he sees in her dark eyes. Even if this paragon did intend to unite herself to someone whose temper was not of the sweetest and who "does not seem to shine in private life", she could not remain in Gibson's house. Did Watson make periodic visits to her lodgings in Winchester and, with the memory of that appealing expression still fresh, win her away from him? It would be a brave man who would thwart such a relentless tycoon; someone who had said "You've done yourself no good this morning, Mr. Holmes, for I have broken stronger men than you. No man ever crossed me and was the better for it." But then Watson was brave – and always drawn to damsels in distress. Particularly the good-looking ones.

Or did the Doctor, as Professor S. C. Roberts suggests, marry Miss Violet de Merville after all? There was a considerable difference in their ages, and Watson knew the name of her real father. A fact which might have inhibited him. He would, however, have had a lot in common with the old soldier who was her assumed father and who had been in Afghanistan. But, although described by Holmes as spiritual, beautiful and with the look of an angel, Miss de Merville is also something of a Fanatic. "As inflexible and remote as a snow image on a mountain." Her refusal to believe in Baron Gruner's murderous past in spite of all the evidence and Holmes' uncharacteristically passionate pleas, her dismissal of one of the Baron's ruined mistresses as someone whose "ravings" she was not compelled to listen to, and which made Holmes "pretty furious myself," as he tells Watson, do not make her a very comfortable kind of person. It is only after she is shown the Baron's Trophy Book containing the names and sordid details of all the women he has ruined that this infuriating woman comes out of her "post-hypnotic" state and breaks off her engagement to him in 'The Illustrious Client'.

Was Watson sympathetic to the loss of the lady's "ecstatic dream," her "living above the earth," before she was so cruelly disillusioned? He was certainly down to earth enough for two. But, after the idyll of his youth with Mary Morstan, one is reluctant to see him in middle-age tied to a spoilt, exacting girl. A female who, at the least crossing of her will, would treat him as she treated everyone who tried to set her right about the Baron. Maybe he did visit General de Merville several times after the investigation was over, and got to know his daughter Violet quite well, even though he never met her during the actual investigation. But, in spite of Roberts' undoubted scholarship, the notion that Watson married such a woman is not one the sensitive reader is prepared to accept without a fight. Rather than the haughty Miss Merville, one could almost wish he had asked Kitty Winter to be his wife. It would explain why Watson never wrote a word or dropped a hint about such a marriage - a doctor careful of his reputation would have to think very hard in those days (and be very much in love) before uniting himself to a fallen woman, even if he were drawn to her by her terrible circumstances. Miss Winter had once been very beautiful. She may even have been refined. But her fall, and subsequent experience of the streets, could only have coarsened her. Watson, naturally, would never have alluded to her past if the two had become man and wife, but perhaps Kitty would have wilted under a life of unremitting respectability – especially if left alone as much as her predecessor was. She may even have become violent, not an unreasonable hypothesis when one recalls what she did to Baron Gruner by throwing vitriol at him.

Watson uncharacteristically becomes quite precise about dates at the time of his brush with the said Baron. He says that in the early days of September 1902, "I was living in my own rooms in Queen Anne Street." But towards the end of June of that year he was still in Baker Street, helping Holmes to solve the mystery of the three Garridebs. So did he marry for the second time between June and September of that year? If this was so, Holmes' "At that time" in 'The Blanched Soldier' is somewhat wide of the mark. It cannot be taken literally.

The Doctor tells his readers that he and Holmes are

together again shortly before the First World War begins. No woman is mentioned, and although Watson feels twenty years younger as a result of this new Adventure, we can only hope that once it was over he had a warm and loving companion to go back to. Even this is problematic, however. At the end of 'His Last Bow', when the two men get together to defeat the Kaiser's spies, though too late for them to prevent a war, it's possible Watson will take a desk job in Whitehall. If so, "104 Berkeley Square ...one of those awful grey London castles which would make a church seem frivolous" could be his home. It is also the home of General de Merville. So perhaps Watson succumbed to his fascination with the Aristocracy and married Miss Violet de Merville after all.

However, a most intriguing problem presents itself in *Sherlock Holmes and the Silk Stocking* where Watson marries a widow from North America called Mrs. Vandeleur. In this 2004 film pastiche, later aired on television at the end of 2008, the lady is a psychologist. The name, in something as far away from the spirit and style of Watson as it is possible to get, is nevertheless one of the many faint echoes from the canon which permeate the entire plot. Mrs.Vandeleur's knowledge of psychology, however, goes way beyond John H. Watson's notion of the *idée fixe*. She carries around a copy of Kraft-Ebbing and is blasé about all manner of perversions.

The more interesting point is that her name has been taken from a character in *The Hound of the Baskervilles*. A name which incidentally is not that character's own. Beryl Garcia, a beautiful woman from *South* America, comes to the North of England with her rascally husband Rodger Baskerville, who has designs on a Baronetcy and Baskerville Hall. But first he tries to run a school (calling himself Vandeleur), ruins it and becomes involved in a fraud. Changing his name again, this time to Stapleton, he flees to Devon and passes his wife off as his sister – who does become a widow when he is sucked into the Great Grimpen Mire. But, although Watson acts very gallantly towards the lady and sympathises with her for having a really brutal and manipulative husband, it's doubtful if she would ever have married him. She and Sir Henry Baskerville have fallen in love. It is more likely that Beryl will wait for and, if he ever does return to Baskerville Hall from the recuperative sea voyage he has gone on with Dr. Mortimer, marry *him*.

'The Mazarin Stone' is almost unique in the canon in having an omniscient narrator: "It was pleasant to Doctor Watson to find himself once more in the untidy room of the first floor in Baker Street." Bored into changing his style of writing, and then regretting it, did Watson put his account of the Mazarin Stone Mystery at the bottom of his old tin trunk and then forget all about it, only to resurrect the piece years later when he was at his wits end what to write? The date of publication is 1921. Billy the pageboy is also there, thirty years after Watson first mentioned him (if it was him) as "the boy in buttons", the one who ushered in Miss Mary Sutherland of 'A Case of Identity' fame published in 1891.

This peculiar intrusion may have been to please the biographer's ever growing band of American readers. Billy is pictured looking particularly efficient in one of Sidney Paget's illustrations for this tale of thwarted love, but otherwise there are only a few passing references to him. In 'The Naval Treaty' he is "the page" and in 'The Yellow Face' Watson calls him "our page." When we get to the case concerning the Mazarin Stone, however, the page's role is enlarged. Holmes asks Watson if he is justified in exposing the boy to the dangers posed by the villainous Count Sylvius and says, "But I can't do without [him] just yet."

Why not? Has Mrs Hudson become too decrepit to announce visitors? Has Billy been trained from the beginning to read out the relevant paragraphs from the newspapers and to look up timetables because Watson can't be away from his wife and his practice all the time, in spite of the impression we get from the canon? Billy *did* have a prominent part in the play based on 'The Speckled Band', but his presence in Baker Street is somewhat shadowy. It would benefit from more explanation than is ever vouchsafed by the Doctor. In two of the investigations where he mentions a page Watson is still sharing rooms with Holmes and able to perform the tasks which may or may not have been assigned to Billy later. By the time of the investigation into the theft of the Mazarin Stone he is a visitor to Baker Street, and Billy seems very much at home there.

Ten years after Watson's Adventure with Charles Augustus Milverton, an investigation in which an accurate description of him causes Holmes to say to Inspector Lestrade that a supposed burglar could almost be the Doctor, a "thick-set chauffeur" sits drinking Imperial Tokay, which has come "from Franz Joseph's special cellar at the Schoenbrunn Palace." He has just helped to capture von Bork, "a man whose talents could hardly be matched among all the devoted agents of the Kaiser." It is the beginning of August 1914, "the most terrible August in the history of the world." Von Bork has plans to escape from Britain before war breaks out, but with inside knowledge gained by posing as a friend of Germany Holmes is in time to prevent this by chloroforming the German. He also manages to recover stolen military secrets hidden in the master-spy's safe. It was touch and go, however. On the way to the rendezvous the "little Ford" he is travelling in is almost run down by a "huge hundred horse-power Benz car" and "But for your excellent driving, Watson, we should have been the very type of Europe under the Prussian juggernaut." In other words, annihilated. Von Bork, gradually recovering consciousness and finding himself trussed up like a chicken, is to be taken to Scotland Yard. "As for you, Watson, you are joining up with your old service, as I understand, so London won't be out of your way."

Perhaps not, but allowing for all the confusion at the start of Watson's army career in 1878 to which regiment was he likely to be attached? In spite of a nation-wide fall in recruitment, due to the formation of Special Reserve and Territorial Force Battalions with greater obligations of service, the Northumberland Fusiliers were able to provide 54 battalions for use in World War One. An unbroken system of trenches, some of them manned by the part-time soldiers of the Territorial Force, stretched through France and Belgium from Switzerland to the English Channel, and on the 26th April 1915 the Northumberland Fusilier Territorials, the first to go into action as a complete brigade, lost 2000 men from their dug-outs in the second battle of Ypres. By 1916 the effort of fighting the War had passed to the men who responded to Kitchener's call of "Your Country Needs You". Because the 16th Battalion of the Northumberland Fusiliers was raised by the efforts of the Newcastle and Gateshead Incorporated Chamber of Commerce it was known as 'The Newcastle Commercials'. Thirteen battalions of what had by then become The Royal

Berkshire Regiment were also in most of the theatres of war from 1914, including France, Flanders, Italy, Salonika, Gallipoli and Mesopotamia. Altogether this particular regiment lost 6,688 men in the War, a faint echo of what happened to it in 1880 when it was known as the 66th Regiment of Foot.

But in 1914 Watson was over sixty and seen by von Bork as "a heavily-built, elderly man with a grey moustache." Is he going to be a Whitehall desk-wallah for the duration of the fighting? That might not suit his need for action, but recruiting posters called for men no older than forty-five to enlist. Holmes probably meant the old Army Medical Service, known since 1898 as the Royal Army Medical Corps, whose School had been relocated in the Capital, and where Watson could become a member of the teaching staff. Whatever the answer, one can be sure he performed his duties as well and as doggedly as he had tried to do for that enigmatic man with whom he is forever associated; and who without him neither could have become such immediately recognised icons of our literary history.

Chapter Twelve: On Being a Foil to a Famous Detective

Conan Doyle wrote a story called *The Doings of Raffles Haw* and his brother-in-law, E.W. Hornung (who wasn't the "Half Mongol, half Slav or whatever the mixture is" that Doyle labelled him, but the fourth son and youngest child of an English mother and a German ironmaster born in Transylvania), asked if he could use the name for stories of his own about an 'Amateur Cracksman'.

Raffles commits crimes not only because he is on his beam ends, but also for the thrill of not being caught. This 'inversion of Sherlock Holmes' has Bunny Manders for a Watson. Bunny is both thrilled and apprehensive about each crime, while Raffles regards them as necessary for his well-being. He has regrets only for his failures. But Manders often brings his own pangs of conscience to the fore – even while continuing to be Raffles' accomplice. It isn't until 'The Gift of the Emperor', that he finally jettisons his hypocritical scruples. His write-ups, however, are livelier. Their endings are both less predictable and more original than Watson's. And he doesn't scruple to show his anger and disappointment when Raffles leaves him in the dark about his plans. Or even completely in the lurch. Sometimes apprehension does get the better of him and he tries to resist Raffles' attempts to inveigle him into crime. Saying, always through set teeth, either "I'm damned if I will!" or "I'll see you damned first!"

In 'Gentlemen and Players' Bunny is anxious to make Miss Melhuish, the Rector's daughter, think well of him. He concedes, in 'The Gift of the Emperor', that Amy Werner has several very good points (including fine eyes), although he admits that he felt "something not unlike jealousy rankling within me" at the amount of time Raffles spent with "such a giddy young school girl." However, he is ('A Thief in the Night') in love with the niece of the Dowager Marchioness of Melrose – who in 'Gentleman and Players' is relieved by Raffles of her extremely valuable diamond and sapphire necklace – and (also in 'Gentlemen and Players') makes a disparaging remark about a young man of the 'exquisite' type with feminine characteristics.

But, while saying that the Holmes/Watson partnership implicitly excludes a sexual content, Owen Dudley Edwards contends that E.W. Hornung produced in Raffles and Bunny an imitation of Holmes and Watson "which is very obviously Homosexual. And a mawkish, cloying, stifling business it is. This is particularly evident in the narrator, Bunny, who becomes very jealous whenever Raffles looks at girls." Edwards also suggests that the pair held rather than shook hands: "To think of having you by the hand again!" says Bunny after Raffles, like Holmes, comes back from the dead in 'No Sinecure'. C.P. Snow, however, although he says there are "homosexual undertones about which Hornung was not in the slightest inhibited", contends that the relationship, while juvenile, was also innocent, the out-pouring of emotion being the reason why Raffles was such a triumph. Nineteenth-century writers had a greater emotional range than their successors, "who have become tight-lipped." In the light of this earlier opinion, Edwards' assertions do seem rather over the top. There is no doubt whatever that Bunny hero-worships Raffles, and repeatedly allows himself to be charmed into being his accomplice. But the writing is in no way mawkish or cloying. Neither is it obviously homosexual – even though Raffles may be loosely based on one of Hornung's friends who was said, euphemistically, to be "burdened by his sexuality."

However, Rohase Piercy in *My Dearest Holmes* contends that the relationship between Holmes and Watson is a homosexual one, the Morstan marriage designed to put readers off the scent. Holmes remarks to Watson, in 'A Case of Identity', "If we could fly out of that window hand in hand, hover over this great city, gently remove the roofs, and peep in at the queer things that are going on, the strange coincidences, the plannings, the cross-purposes, the wonderful chains of events, working through generations, and leading to the most outré results, it would make all fiction with its conventionalities and foreseen conclusions most stale and unprofitable."

A poorly drawn illustration in *The Strand Magazine* for 'The Illustrious Client' appears to show Watson in bed with Holmes. In reality they are lying on adjacent couches in a Turkish bath-house. In another investigation they are obliged to take a double-bedded room "which was the best that the little country inn could do for us." And when in another investigation Holmes comes to the bedside and asks an awakened Watson, "Would you be afraid to sleep in the same room with a lunatic, a man with softening of the brain, an idiot whose mind has lost its grip?" is this just to enhance the drama? Unfortunately Watson's stalwart "Not in the least" and Holmes "Ah, that's lucky" is followed by "and not another word would he utter that night." Was Watson curious enough to question Holmes into the small hours and go without any more sleep himself? The whole episode suggests that even if they shared a room their beds were single at any rate.

They were alone together in a bedroom in 'The Man with the Twisted Lip', and again in 'The Speckled Band'. But on the first occasion Holmes "wandered about the room collecting pillows from his bed and cushions from the sofa and armchairs". He is constructing an "Eastern divan" and will sit cross-legged on it all night. In the second case the two men wait, fully clothed, to go to the rescue of Helen Stoner. Such examples of togetherness don't appear to be sufficient evidence of what was at that time forbidden love. According to Terry Manners, discussing the television series and writing of the beginnings and endings of the Holmes/Watson investigations, these revealed "extraordinary details of Victorian friendship between two men without having any sexual overtones. It was all "Just friendship, uncomplicated in its nature, something that perhaps [our] fast-moving world lost sight of." Strong and emotional friendships between men were easily accepted during the nineteenth century. "Writers could celebrate one man's love for another without any thought of impropriety crossing their own or their readers' minds. In fact there is a striking contrast between the prurient delicacy in force between respectable men and women and the uninhibited behaviour allowed between men. Adolescent brothers and sisters might be forbidden to enter each other's bedrooms. But no one in their senses thought it improper for men and boys to bathe naked or relieve themselves in company." Neither were strong and emotional friendships between women taboo or Charles Dickens and Wilkie Collins, for example, could not have written as they did. Watson can describe young men in far more rapturous terms than is possible today for a heterosexual male to think of doing. And even Sherlock Holmes uses the description "comely" about the young James McCarthy in 'The Boscombe Valley Mystery'. So is it a mistake to say, as Mark Campbell does, that even taking into consideration the change of literary style over the past century it is difficult to avoid the conclusion that Scott Eccles is homosexual? This elderly man is a bachelor who, in his own words, cultivates a large number of friends. At a dinner one evening in Kensington he makes the acquaintance of a much younger fellow, a Spaniard who speaks perfect English, has charming manners, and is "as good looking a man as ever I saw in my life." The Spaniard appears to take a fancy to the older man and invites him to his house. A queer one to find in the heart of Surrey, as Garcia himself remarks, where a male servant does all the housework and another male "half-breed" the cooking. Scott Eccles says to Holmes that things became even more odd later on when he came down to breakfast and found his host had disappeared. If any of this shows that Eccles was homosexual what does it tell us about Doyle? That in spite of two marriages and five children he was a latent homosexual, expressing his feelings subconsciously? He greatly admired Oscar Wilde and said that "The monstrous happening" which came upon him was "Pathological, needing a hospital rather than a prison."

Be that as it may Martin Fido says, when comparing Hornung's anti-establishment figures with Doyle's two creations, that there is a "brisk bachelor sexlessness [in] Holmes and Watson's affection for each other." In his opinion it is quite unlike Bunny's feeling for Raffles, with its "queasy and faintly homo-erotic tone." Bunny, who was Raffles' fag at school, "mingles, in almost equal measure, shock at his friend's apparent amorality and completely submissive hero-worship for his daring." This is to misread the text. The hero worship is not completely submissive. There are times when Bunny absolutely refuses to aid Raffles, who has to use all his charm to win him round. Neither is the tone queasy. Better to say that it's inevitable, given the pair's relationship at school –a relationship which Raffles cynically exploits to the full. And can one ignore 'The Fate of Faustina', in which Raffles relates the details of his doomed love affair to Bunny? A Bunny who, far from being jealous, evinces the greatest sympathy. But homosexual or not, Raffles and Bunny are not two imitations of Holmes and Watson gone to the bad. Raffles is no Moriarty and Bunny no Colonel Sebastian Moran. They were, however, sufficiently exciting to provoke imitations. For example, Arsène Lupin is a Gentleman Thief invented by the French writer Maurice Leblanc. At the outset of his career he specialises in burglary. Although he later turns to detection, it was as a confidence trickster that he achieved his greatest popularity, inspiring G K. Chesterton in his creation of Flambeau, the convict turned crime *fighter* in association with another of Chesterton's creations, Father Brown.

R. Austin Freeman, in collaboration with John Pitcairn and using the pseudonym 'Clifford Ashdown' invented the rascally Romney Pringle but, as Robert S. Paul writes, "To make a hero of the criminal is to reverse the moral law, which is after all based on common sense, for crime is not in fact generous but mean." A sentiment Conan Doyle might easily have agreed with. According to Hugh Greene, however, Freeman's other creation (the law-abiding Doctor Thorndyke) is a more realistic solver of crimes than Holmes. He has Doctor Jervis as a Watson who helps him with his investigations and writes them up. Jervis also responds in much the same way as Watson does when Holmes mentions danger: "Thank you," said I, somewhat huffily. "I don't see what risk there is, but if any exists I claim the right to share it." Which is very like Watson at his most determined in 'Charles Augustus Milverton'.

Arthur Morrison's 'Martin Hewitt' appeared initially in *The Strand Magazine* soon after Sherlock Holmes seemed to have gone over the Reichenbach Falls and the editor could expect no more accounts of his exploits. Since Morrison's detective stories are interestingly plotted, well-crafted and, like Watson's accounts, illustrated by the London artist Sidney Paget, one would expect them to be almost as popular. Morrison had written gripping first-hand novels of the East End of London, including the minor classic *A Child of the Jago*. He also created his own inversion of the form with a crooked 'hero', Dorrington. But the Hewitt stories suffer from straining after Watson's style and content. Hewitt exchanges pleasantries with the policeman Plummer, and with other characters in each investigation. But the interplay between two complementary personalities like Holmes and Watson is muted, and sometimes missing altogether. As Chesterton says, they [Holmes and Watson] are the only two fictional characters to have passed into the life and language of the country and be familiar to both the cultured and the uncultured, "breaking out of the book as a chicken breaks out of an egg."

Hewitt is aware of the jealousy which the professional policeman feels towards the private and the consulting detective and plays his cards very close to his chest. Readers are given clues which might help, but there's sometimes nobody there to ask the questions which would give them a lead as they go along. For example 'Brett' doesn't appear at all, by name at least, in some of the investigations. Although he does materialise at the very end of 'The Case of Laker, Absconded' to ask a few questions, and to mention 'The Stanway Cameo Mystery' in which he seems to have played a part. However, an earlier investigation, the third in the series ('The Case of Laker, Absconded' being the twelfth) and called 'The Case of Mr. Fogatt', has already made everything clear to the reader. Mr. Brett is a journalist, not sharing rooms with Hewitt but living in the same set of chambers where the detective has his office. This makes it easy for the two men to meet socially to discuss the crimes Hewitt is trying to solve, and the following passages do have a certain familiarity about them: "Almost the only dogmatism that Martin Hewitt permitted himself in regard to his professional method was one on the matter of accumulative probabilities. Often when I have remarked upon the apparently trivial nature of the clues by which he allowed himself to be guided – sometimes, to all seeming, in the very face of all likelihood – he has replied that two trivialities, pointing in the same direction, became at once by their mere agreement no trivialities at all, but enormously important considerations." And "It is now a good number of years back since the loss of the famous Stanway Cameo made its sensation, and the only person who had the least interest in keeping the real facts of the case secret has now been dead for some time, leaving neither relatives nor other representatives. Therefore no harm will be done in making the inner history of the case public; on the contrary, it will afford an opportunity of vindicating the professional reputation of Hewitt, who is supposed to have completely failed to make anything of the mystery surrounding the case." A small mystery of another kind is suddenly solved. Brett is revealed as a Watson figure earning his living partly by writing up Hewitt's cases, and happy to reveal he's nowhere near as clever. But in several instances he is elsewhere while Hewitt is working on a case and only hears about it later. Mr. Foggatt is later found, shot dead with his own revolver, alone in a locked room it is impossible to get into or out of. But Hewitt says he *knows* another man was in there with him. It isn't suicide but murder.

Morrison's Brett is as puzzled as his Watson counterpart, even though he has seen the room. But Hewitt, after taking him through a detailed description of the crime, refuses to enlighten him any further saying, "You don't deserve it. Think, and don't mention the subject again till you have at least one guess to make. The thing stares you in the face – you see it, you remember it, and yet you *won't* see it. I won't encourage your slovenliness of thought, my boy, by telling you what you can know for yourself if you like." This is Holmes at his most patronising, and recalls a conversation between him and Watson in 'A Scandal in Bohemia' in which the Great Detective accuses his foil of 'seeing' but not 'observing'. "The distinction is clear. For example, you have frequently seen the steps which lead up from the hall to this room." Watson agrees he has, hundreds of times, but says he has no idea how many there are. Says Sherlock, "Quite so! You have not observed. And yet you have seen. That is just my point. Now, I know there are seventeen steps, because I have both seen and observed."

Six weeks after the Foggatt murder Hewitt asks Brett to dinner at Luzatti's, his favourite eating house just off Coventry Street. This is similar to Holmes' Marcini's, where he stopped for a "little supper" with Watson on their way to a concert. Once the two men are settled, Hewitt strikes up a conversation with a young man he pretends to have met by chance. Slim and decidedly athletic, there's nevertheless something singular about this person's teeth. He's a keen amateur cyclist who has had an accident. Hewitt adroitly pockets part of an apple which the young man has been chewing for dessert. When he and Brett are safely back in the latter's lodgings, Hewitt says that he has earlier examined a piece of apple from the murdered man's room and found that it bore marks of very irregular teeth. "I oiled it over and, rushing down to my rooms, where I always have a little Plaster of Paris handy for such work, took a mould of the part where the teeth had made the clearest marks. I then returned the apple to its place, for the police to use if they thought fit. Looking at my mould, it was plain that the person who had bitten the apple had lost two teeth [and that] the other teeth were irregular in size. Now the dead man had, as I saw, a very excellent set of false teeth, regular and sharp, with none missing. Therefore it was plain that somebody else had been eating the apple."

Hewitt remarks that it is unlikely a man of Foggatt's age would munch an unpeeled apple like a schoolboy whether or not his teeth were irregular, and the unwelcome visitor must have been athletic to climb out of the window and successfully grab the edge of some guttering to make his escape. Taking the second bit of apple, the piece obtained from the restaurant, Brett says that Hewitt again oiled it, put a little of his plaster of Paris on a sheet of newspaper, took some water from a carafe with which to make a paste, dipped his stolen specimen into it, and in a little while rapidly pulled off a hard mould. "The parts corresponding to the merely broken pieces in the apple were, of course, dissimilar; but as to the teeth marks, the impressions [from the two pieces of apple] were identical."

One is irresistibly reminded of Hans Gross, Patrick Heron Watson and their uses of plaster casts, Watson's mention of Holmes' monograph on the subject, and how dentistry is used in modern-day forensic science. Mouths are very individual, and dentures survive fire and flood as well as the grave. Corpses still retaining their own teeth are x-rayed and the results compared with ones taken in life. Teeth which have not yet erupted, unfilled cavities invisible when the person lived, all help towards identification after death. Where there are no dental records family photographs can often provide clues towards the identity of the murdered person by showing any irregularities in the formation of the teeth. As Judy Williams says in her book *The Modern Sherlock Holmes – An Introduction to Forensic Science Today*, "It is particularly poignant that, because people are usually smiling broadly, wedding photographs are useful for this sort of comparison."

To put Brett's role beyond doubt, he writes a preamble to 'The Ivy Cottage Mystery' and later plays an even more Watsonian part in it saying, "I had been working double tides for a month: at night on my morning paper as usual; and in the morning on an evening paper as locum tenens for another man who was taking a holiday. This was an exhausting plan of work...I turned up at the headquarters of my own paper at ten in the evening, and by the time I had seen the editor, selected a subject, written my leader, corrected the slips, chatted, smoked and so on, and cleared off, it was very usually one o'clock." Before the days of computer-generated copy, "slips" (of paragraph sized, very thin paper) were used, one for the reporter and one for the printer, a method which was still being employed as late as 1988 by some provincial newspapers.

During the time Brett has been so busy an acquaintance of his is murdered and the investigation of the crime given to Hewitt, who asks, "Didn't you say you knew the man?" Brett replies that he did, but only by sight. "He was a boarder in a house at Chelsea where I stayed before I started chambers." Hewitt then says something which serves to fix Brett definitely as his Watson: "Do you feel particularly interested in the case? I mean, if you've nothing better to do, would you come with me?" Brett's answer to this is that he would be very glad as "I was in some doubt what to do with myself. Shall you start at once?" Apart from the absence of the 'old service revolver' we might almost be listening to Holmes and Watson in their shared sitting room in Baker Street before they jump into a hansom, grab a growler or hurry to catch a train. However, these passages from Morrison highlight the difficulties he had in trying to replace Watson. He couldn't be completely original when what the readers, the editor and the publisher of the *Strand* desperately wanted was a second Holmes and Watson. But the effort to provide something sufficiently like them to please, at the same time as it was unlike enough to please the author and make him feel he was creating something of his own, proved too much. Morrison, in spite of his praiseworthy efforts, produced neither fish nor fowl. He was no Watson, and the readers felt Hewitt was no Holmes. Circulation had not been visibly increased or even sustained, and Morrison's second set of Hewitt stories went to *The Windsor Magazine.* Where they may have escaped unwelcome comparison with what was already becoming an iconic set of characters.

Baroness Orczy, as well as conceiving the idea of the Scarlet Pimpernel, and later the less successful professional female detective Lady Molly of Scotland Yard, has as a male detective 'The Man in the Corner'. He sits in an A.B.C. teashop in Norfolk Street, Strand, continually fidgeting with a piece of string, tying and untying it as he goes through the salient points of his narrative. A 'lady journalist' named Polly Burton, who has had wind of an investigation, meets him there regularly for more enlightenment. Although the string-lover appears to be the ultimate in passivity, it turns out he has visited the towns where various murders, completely baffling to everyone else, have taken place and has already solved them. The journalist is more sceptical than Watson and her objections, made of course on behalf of the reader, gradually reveal the plots. She, like Watson, writes up the stories; but unlike Watson gets her information without so much as moving from her chair. It turns out that not only has The Man in the Corner been to each location, he has managed to get into the police court, heard all the evidence and summed up the defendant: "I succeeded – I generally do – in securing one of the front seats among the audience, and was already comfortably installed in my place in court when through the trapdoor I saw the head of the prisoner emerge."

He is dismissive of the regular police force. "Personally I don't wonder the police were completely at sea. If a member of that highly estimable force happened to be as clever as the clever author of that forged will, we should have very few undetected crimes in this country." The 'lady journalist', with some sarcasm of her own, says that's why she is always trying to persuade the man sitting opposite her with his tangled string and his snapshots of all the people concerned in a case to give "our poor ignorant police" the benefit of his "great insight and wisdom." The Man in the Corner replies blandly that he is an amateur, and it is only the ingenuity of the crime which interests him, which sounds very much like Sherlock Holmes.

Another woman, this time definitely a Holmes figure, appears in detective stories by the American Hugh C. Weir. Madelyn Mack, "The delightful, golden-haired and beautiful college girl who had to earn her own living", is as clever, as evasive and as maddening as Sherlock at his worst. She follows his methods and breaks out in expressions which would do credit to him as a model, saying, "I am not a murderess! I refer to my dissecting room experiences." Like Holmes, Miss Mack has "a grip of steel" and is given to staging dramatic dénouements. She also has her Watson. Miss Noraker ("Nora") is on hand to say things like "I'm afraid I don't quite follow you. There is nothing at all out of the ordinary that I can catch." She is pleased to do some sleuthing on her own account, and amazed to find that on one occasion her friend isn't in Jamaica but New York. In other words, like poor Watson, she doesn't always know where Madelyn is, where she has been or what she has been getting up to. Nevertheless, again like Watson, Nora is perfectly willing to go with her anywhere without warning – and at any time of the day or night.

Her reference to "The tyrant of our city editor's desk" implies that Nora too, like Baroness Orczy's 'Lady Journalist', will write up Madelyn's cases in the best Watsonian manner. First, though, she must ask the questions which will clear up one or two little points. Points which reasonably attentive readers may have already worked out for themselves: "Why did [the murderer] bring you back a blank sheet of paper when you dispatched him on your errand?" Madelyn replies that there was nothing else he could do. She had sent the man on a false message and arranged that the reply should be a blank piece of note-paper enclosed in an envelope for him to bring back. This was so that she could search the miscreant's room undisturbed. When Nora asks, "And what was the quarrel that the servant girl, Anna, heard in the Duffield library?" Miss Mack replies condescendingly that it wasn't a quarrel.

The murdered man, a Senator, used a phonograph to prepare his speeches "and some of them are rather fiery." Simple when explained, as Watson would say, but a neat end to a clever story.

Lord Peter Wimsey, Dorothy L. Sayers' aristocratic detective, has as his foil a servant called Bunter – his former batman turned general factotum. Bunter stops short of writing up his employer's investigations. But he is very useful, for example, in the dark room. Acting on his own hunch in *Unnatural Death*, he brings to the attention of Wimsey and the police his photograph of a set of fingerprints found on a wine glass. They are the same as a set found on a cheque. The murderer has tried but failed to establish a double identity and, hey presto, after a lot of quite remarkable shenanigans (including Wimsey's deliberate attempt to make love to a lesbian) is brought to justice.

In *Have His Carcase* Bunter is given the job of shadowing a suspect. Jumping on and off buses, taking a night's lodging in a series of seedy London doss houses, sometimes even travelling in the same vehicle as his quarry, he finally decides taxis would be safer. In "a suit of horrible cheap serge, which it gave him acute agony to wear" and "a disgusting bowler of curly shape and heavy quality" he continued the chase, each day modifying his disguise by changing his style of hat or wearing a "subfusc overcoat." Coming to the conclusion that "the perpetual presence of a man with a paper parcel [of clothes] would alarm the fugitive [he] had relieved his arm and his mind by depositing the loathly bowler under the table in an eating-house."

It can be seen from this that Bunter is, unlike Watson and more like Sexton Blake's side-kick Tinker, given quite a lot to do - and does it most efficiently. This may be because he doesn't have to face continual put-downs from his detective who, unlike Holmes, finds his help extremely useful and frequently tells him so. But Robert Graves says that Lord Peter, based on the "lackadaisical" Sir Percy Blakeney ('The Scarlet Pimpernel'), "outclassed all other detective heroes at least in the fantastic complications of his cases." Which must have exercised his former batman's ingenuity to the full. The books also became hooks on which to hang dissertations on various subjects which interested the author. Readers were bemused by what was then uncommon knowledge among the masses, and caught up in a net of tremendous erudition. It's done less obviously today, and with less condescension. The material isn't so obtuse, and incorporated more naturally into the narrative - an example being Emma Lathen's wonderful detective story about American hockey, *Murder Without Icing*. Being a little more sophisticated, however, and generally a little more educated, readers are often aware that the incidental information the detective writer incorporates into his or her tale is there not only to make the whole work more rounded but also to delay a dénouement.

Interestingly enough, the so-called 'Queen of Crime' told us nothing except what was relevant to the puzzles she was presenting in her detective novels. Agatha Christie wrote resolutely of her own milieu, one which she knew would be acceptable to her readers. The world of servants, tea on the lawn and seemingly unalterable middle-class mores. The only concessions she made when things did begin to alter was an off-hand reference to "the new estate on the edge of the village" or "the difficulties one has these days in getting someone to come in to help with the heavy work". There's a reference to "young men, practically only boys still, taking a lot of drugs and going wild and rushing about, shooting a lot of people for nothing at all, asking a girl in a pub to have a drink with them and then they see her home and next day her body's found in a ditch." But this is in a late book, written when Christie was in her eighties. However, the attempt to be 'modern' jars. It doesn't quite gel with the rest of *Elephants Can Remember*. Fans are glad to get back to the unreal world, where common girls continue to be dumped in colonels' libraries and distressing murders take place in country vicarages. This was a formula which worked for everybody. The high recognised themselves, and the low lived in vicarious enjoyment of what, in their heart of hearts, they may not really have cared to join. But apart from the odd remark 'for colour' in her stories, for example about murder on archaeological digs, Christie makes no attempt to 'educate' the reader, remaining faithful to what Graves rather puzzling calls, in view of her somewhat simplistic prose, "the romantic cumbersome-English style of the early twenties."

Kingsley Amis, in an Introduction to a 1974 edition of *The Memoirs of Sherlock Holmes,* says that the relationship between Holmes and Watson is similar to that of Rex Stout's Nero Wolfe and his Watson, Archie Goodwin. A relationship which "haunts the memory after the various unravellings have begun to fade." But physically Wolfe must be one of the laziest detectives on record, and it is quite likely that he is based on Sherlock's brother Mycroft. It's Archie who does all the running about, bringing the results of his activity to Nero to sort out and so solve the crimes. But, although this particular detective may owe his inception to Mycroft Holmes, Nero is even more passive. Mycroft does at least venture out to help his brother at least twice; or three times if one counts the disguised expert coachman in 'The Final Problem'.

August Derleth's detective, Solar Pons, has Doctor Lyndon Parker as his foil and treats him in much the same way as Holmes does Watson. Indeed, apart from a slight faltering in style occasionally, we might almost be listening to the two occupants of Baker Street. Pons, however, lives elsewhere and wears an Inverness cape rather than an ulster. But his 'adventures' are remarkably similar to those of Holmes; and the scheme of what the noted Sherlockian, Vincent Starrett, calls Derleth's 'sequels' to the canon is, as he says, "more than just a little reminiscent; it is frankly borrowed. Dr. Lyndon Parker returns to London just in time to make [the] book possible. Solar Pons, The Sherlock Holmes of Praed Street, is even then looking about him for some amiable fellow to act as his Watson; he loses no time in persuading the doctor to share the Pontine lodgings." The rest of the cast also loses no time in coming on stage: Mrs. Johnson, their 'long-suffering' landlady, a substitute Moriarty in the shape of the villainous Baron Ennesfred Kroll and, in one tale at least, The Praed Street Irregulars - obviously a copy of the Baker Street variety. And there is, naturally, the endless creating and indexing of hundreds of scrapbooks.

But, as Vincent Starrett says in his introduction to *The Adventures of Solar Pons* (Futura Publications, 1976), "One likes the author's trick of using the exact words and phrases of the original sagas, when it suits his purpose, and greets with a smile of pleasure such familiar lines as 'Dark waters, Parker, dark waters' [and] 'Come, Parker! The game is afoot." Pons even mentions, "like the exasperating Watson", cases he is not going to expand upon. Which is intriguing enough to be acceptable.

This use of what has gone before, of course, fits in well

with the classical model of detective writing, which was (and is) extremely conservative and created to perpetuate the myth of a basically well-ordered society. It was *The Face on the Cutting-Room Floor* by 'Cameron McCabe' (the German Sexologist E. W. Borneman) which finally caused this comforting tradition to fall to the ground. The supposed investigator's motives are skewed, his policeman-antagonist's actions are suspect, and the reader confronted with the possibility of multiple endings. Indeed, we are told there need be no definitive ending to any detective story.

Borneman was making sarcastic remarks about Doyle's detective stories and the Holmes/Watson partnership as early as 1935. Traditional methods of detection (for example identifying cigarette ash found on the drawing room carpet or in the woods) were no good because there were always an unlimited number of possibilities from which to make faulty deductions. Clues could be left out or misinterpreted; and in any case no result was ever foolproof. It was the death-knell of classicism.

Chapter Thirteen: On Being a Foil (Continued)

Watson says of Holmes in *A Study in Scarlet*, "I had already observed that he was as sensitive to flattery on the score of his art as any girl could be of her beauty."

So, given the traditional relationship between the two attributes, did Agatha Christie imitate Sherlock and Watson by accident or design? Peter Costello says, in *The Real World of Sherlock Holmes*, that "She owed him [Conan Doyle] a great deal. After all, Poirot and Hastings are based on Holmes and Watson; her use of detail owes much to Watson; and both had written books on and about Dartmoor."

This is in spite of what Christie herself made public. Having decided (while working in a dispensary during the First World War) that she would write a detective story, she then began casting around for a suitable subject and says in her *Autobiography*, "There was Sherlock Holmes, the one and only – I should never be able to emulate him!" But this didn't stop her having a character say, in *Death in the Clouds*, "Personally I myself think the Sherlock Holmes stories grossly overrated. The fallacies – the really amazing fallacies that there are in those stories..." Neither did it stop her when it came to inventing Chief-Inspector James Japp. Hastings describes him as "a little, sharp, dark ferret-faced man." Watson writes, "One little sallow, rat-faced, dark-eyed fellow was introduced to me as Mr. Lestrade." The parallel is obvious.

When Christie suddenly disappeared from home in 1926, Conan Doyle suggested that an appeal to the spirit world, might solve the problem of where she had gone. In 1929, when she came to write her series of spoofs called *Partners in Crime,* Agatha took her revenge for what she saw as unjustified interference. In 'The Missing Lady' she guyed Watson's story of Lady Frances Carfax, giving her version of it what Costello calls "a farcical twist" and allowing her character, 'Tommy', to suggest to his wife, 'Tuppence', that perhaps this particular tale need not be written up at all because "It has no distinctive features." Perhaps she was still smarting from Doyle's intervention three years after it happened. But any reservations she may have about him or his creation (including the foil he invented for his detective) didn't prevent Christie from appropriating many aspects of that foil in her search for one of her own. After deciding to model *her* detective on some Belgian refugees ("We had quite a colony living in the parish of Tor") all that was needed then was to "give him his Watson". But did she have to steal quite so much of the Doctor's clothing, even if Christie admits that she, along with many other detective story writers, was working in the Sherlock Holmes tradition at that time?

This assertion is partly supported by Michael Cox (*Victorian Tales of Mystery and Detection*) who says, "Throughout the 1890s and into the early twentieth Century the short detective story could not rid itself of Baker Street. In many cases, at least to begin with, it had no wish to do so: public appetite appeared to be insatiable and there was no shortage of publishers to satisfy it." According to a piece of doggerel, written by 'Sagittarius' (Mrs. Katzin-Miller) for *The London Mystery Magazine*, Sherlock was at the head of a "lynx-eyed procession" – with an endless succession of detectives following his trail and succeeding where the Yard failed: "Did he guess that he'd started, that wizard sardonic, something that would not stop?" *The Strand Magazine* had many rivals, and so did Holmes.

But Watson also had a very obvious rival. Hastings,

called by Emma Lathen "An all-purpose stooge", has (like the other old soldier) been invalided out of the services. He is given a war pension for a short time and has spent a few "depressing months" in a convalescent home. At a loose end, he tells a friend (in *The Mysterious Affair at Styles*) "I've always had a hankering to be a detective." The friend asks if he means the real thing, Scotland Yard, or Sherlock Holmes? Hastings' reply to this is, "Oh, Sherlock Holmes by all means. But really, seriously, I'm awfully drawn to it."

Watson says (in 'The Speckled Band') "I had no keener pleasure than in following Holmes in his professional investigations." Later on, in *The Hound of the Baskervilles*, he is delighted to be given the opportunity to do some sleuthing by himself. Just as he does in 'The Illustrious Client', where Holmes uses him to distract Baron Gruner and which he calls "my own little adventure." According to his account of this case, Watson also gets more chance than usual to play the doctor when the Baron is suddenly horribly injured. But, although he says he employed oil and cotton wadding to treat his patient, both of which might be available in a private house, it's difficult to see where the "hypodermic of morphia" sprung from. Watson was posing as Doctor Hill Barton. "You may as well be a medical man, since that is a part you can play without duplicity," says Sherlock. However, on this occasion Watson is acting as an expert in ceramics. It's highly unlikely he would be carrying his 'little black bag' with him. He muffs the pose, of course, and has to be rescued by Holmes. But, as Roger Johnson suggests, how many people could convincingly sustain it for as long as the Doctor did, with only 24 hours notice and in the presence of a genuine expert? Poirot considers Hastings is not doing things properly either, after giving him a chance to show his mettle by allowing him to work alone in the story called 'Hunter's Lodge'.

Like his earlier counterpart, Hastings is susceptible to women and falls in and out of love during Poirot's investigations. But, in the same way as Watson finally carries off Mary Morstan in *The Sign of Four*, so Hastings marries a young acrobat he meets in *Murder on the Links*. Both women are amazingly accommodating. Dulcie Duveen is willing to accept almost single-handedly the responsibilities of running a ranch in Argentina while her husband is thousands of miles away helping to catch criminals. He mixes her up with his sister-in-law Bella in much the same way as Watson's wife absentmindedly calls her husband James on one occasion.

As for her, every time Holmes crooks a finger she is more than willing to send her husband off on yet another Adventure. When a telegram arrives asking for help in solving 'The Boscombe Valley Mystery' her only comment is, "Anstruther will do your work for you. You have been looking a little pale lately. I think a change of air would do you good, and you are always so interested in Mr. Sherlock Holmes' cases." Watson says that he really doesn't know what to do as he has "a fairly long list [of patients] at present." In reality, of course, he is dying to be off. One can't help being reminded of Hastings who takes Poirot away for "a change of air" in 'The Jewel Robbery at the Grand Metropolitan'.

We are not told how Mrs. Watson met her death, and there is a similar reticence about Dulcie Hastings. Watson's only comment (in 'The Empty House') is that in some manner "he [Holmes] had heard of my sad bereavement, and his sympathy was shown in his manner rather than in his words." Hastings merely says of poor, harassed Dulcie, so much younger than himself and with all those responsibilities, "She died as she would have wished, with no long drawn out suffering, no feebleness of old age." In both instances their respective detectives advise that activity is the best antidote to grief. Holmes says, "I have a piece of work for us both tonight which, if we can bring it to a successful conclusion, will in itself justify a man's life on this planet." In *Curtain: Poirot's Last Case* Hastings is told he must be the eyes, ears and even the knees of the now wheelchair-bound Poirot.

He indignantly declines listening at keyholes. But we're sure he will do so if Poirot insists on it. And there are other points besides work where the two foils resemble each other. Hastings has a "speaking countenance." Poirot will tell him nothing because his friend will then sit with his face saying plainly, "This is – this that I am looking at – is the murderer." Sixty years earlier Holmes said to Watson that among the Doctor's many talents "dissimulation finds no place." Both foils are being presented as equally ingenuous.

There has been some speculation that Mary Watson died in childbirth. At twenty-seven when she first met Watson ("A sweet age" says the Doctor, in graceful compliment to Doyle's first wife Louise at the time of their wedding) she was somewhat older than average for a Victorian bride. By 1894, when Holmes returned to London after a three year absence, she could have been well into her thirties by Watson's reckoning. This would make childbirth even more hazardous than it already was for younger women. Contraceptive methods were known, especially to doctors, and some of the literature was explicit. But it circulated in an underground manner, silently tolerated until the trial of Bradlaugh and Besant – when a pamphlet published in

America was distributed by them in Britain and led to both being prosecuted for obscenity.

Of course, Watson in his role of gallant gentleman and honourable officer in *The Sign of Four*, expressed relief that he could propose (once the Agra Treasure Chest went into the river) without the imputation of trying to marry a woman immensely richer than he was. But what did his wife do all day? Dulcie Hastings at least had a ranch to run. Thanks to the Married Women's Property Acts of 1870 and 1882 Mary Watson had the use of her own money, and was not regarded, as married women had been in the past, as her husband's chattel. But one doesn't get the impression from the Doctor that she occupied her time in frequent shopping sprees. Did she pass hours sitting on charitable committees, which was something a middle-class woman was almost expected to do (especially if she had no children or other pressing domestic duties)? Maybe she marched with the Women's Franchise League, the forerunner of the far more militant Suffragette Movement. Did she, in desperation, become a New Woman and join The Rational Dress Society, whose aim was to promote a style of clothing for women that was both healthy and more comfortable – as well as giving freedom to ride bicycles. A freedom which was the signal for other more important and, some would say, invidious freedoms? If Watson was as conservative as he appeared to be, or if he habitually over-compensated for something shady in his background, such activities would have made him very uneasy.

Did Mary help her husband entertain as part of a medical man's social obligations? John H. was rarely able to persuade Holmes to leave Baker Street. But what about his old friend Hayter from Afghanistan? Did the Colonel come up for an occasional weekend? Did Thurston, who sometimes played billiards with the Doctor, bring his wife to supper? Did the Watsons frequent the theatre? More often than not, he is too tired at the end of the day for anything other than snoozing by his own fireside. This may be because he makes suspiciously heavy weather of his doctoring or because, without the excitement of the chase, his avowed laziness kicks in. Might one, therefore, hazard a guess that poor Mary Morstan simply died of boredom?

Although Doyle's work profited by the interplay between two complementary characters able to function in self-contained units, one of his own criticisms of the form was that it could become too rigid. However, any attempt to broaden it out would result in the loss of that interplay, and change the structure which was proving so advantageous. He did try to open things up in his second investigation, which he may have thought would be his last, by introducing a wife for Watson and getting him away from Baker Street. But if the relationship between the two men was to continue in the same way as it started then Watson would have to be given excuses for continually coming back into the frame. His début in *The Strand Magazine* with 'A Scandal in Bohemia' began something which would occupy his creator for nearly forty years, and the literary world for more than a century after that. The most interesting aspect of each Adventure was the interaction between the personalities of the two men, only partly followed by the investigation itself. Which meant that everything had to be subordinated to this if the formula was to continue to work. The above speculations about Mary Morstan show the extent to which Doyle did subordinate everything about her. He just couldn't be bothered to develop this character in a way which would make her credible or even too believable. In the end it was easier to kill her off. Christie makes much the same mistake about Dulcie Duveen. Marrying Hastings to this young woman, she gets rid of him for a while. But, needing to bring him back, also finds it easier to dispose of the wife. Not developing characters too much is, of course, part of the classical tradition of detective fiction which Christie inherited. If characters are too rounded, and in a sympathetic way, we don't want them to be the guilty party. According to H. R. F. Keating ('Agatha Lives On') in *Agatha Christie First Lady of Crime*, by making none of the characters the person you *want* to have done it, the reader is left with the "formulaic fun" of the puzzle. We become gripped by trying to guess who the murderer could be, and don't wish to be distracted by anything more than the most superficial of relationships.

To take the matter further, Watson's accounts centre so much on Holmes, and are so coloured by his intense admiration for him, that nearly everything is subordinated to Sherlock and his investigations. Apart from the main protagonists, who have interesting foibles and are placed in interesting situations, we are not told enough about anyone else to become personally involved or overly sympathetic towards them and their troubles. This applies particularly to Mary Watson, of whom it would be natural to know more. However, Watson's accounts are not, unlike Christie's, particularly cryptic. Their main interest lies in how Holmes will react to and deal with investigations while throwing out esoteric information, writing no end of monographs on (usually) abstruse subjects and studying obscure palimpsests. Drug addiction and the violin playing also play their part, and are perhaps the reason why city clerks may (or may not) have been dismayed enough to put on black arm-bands when they thought Holmes had gone over the

Falls. In the end the man mattered more than the mystery.

It comes as some surprise to Watson to discover, in 'The Greek Interpreter', that Holmes has a brother, Mycroft. This gentleman possesses "a faculty of observation and a facility for deduction" greater even than Sherlock's own. But Mycroft is indolent and prefers a quiet life. Poirot, we aren't surprised to learn therefore, also has an equally retiring and indolent brother whose powers greatly exceed those of the little Belgian detective. The only difference is that, whereas Mycroft is seven years older than Sherlock, Achille and Hercule are twins. To emphasis the point that all these names are even by today's standards distinctly odd, in *The Labours of Hercules* (first published as late as 1947) a character laughingly imagines, when speaking to Poirot, "Your mother and the late Mrs Holmes sewing little garments or knitting." And at the same time musing over names: "Achille, Hercule, Sherlock, Mycroft."

Later, speaking to a doctor, Poirot surveys a room littered with cigarette ends and broken wine glasses and says facetiously, "*Mon cher* Watson, I deduce that there has been here a party!" Christie appropriates the names of Doyle's characters only to sneer. This is obvious from the jeering reference to jewels hidden in plaster busts, and a dog which is taught to "die for Sherlock Holmes" and then, more emphatically, to "*die for M. Hercule Poirot.*" Holmes describes the murderer in 'The Boscombe Valley Mystery as "A tall man, left-handed, limps with the right leg, wears thick-soled shooting boots and a grey cloak, smokes Indian cigars, uses a cigar-holder and carries a blunt penknife in his pocket." An exasperated Poirot says to an impatient Hastings, "The crime was committed by a man of medium height with red hair and a cast in the left eye. He limps slightly on the right foot and has a mole just below the shoulder-blade. *Mon ami,* what will you? You fix me with the look of dog-like devotion and demand of me a pronouncement à la Sherlock Holmes. Now for the truth – I do not know what the man looks like, nor where he lives, nor how *to set hands on him.*"

This outburst, together with remarks such as "Sherlock Holmes v. the local police, is that it?" and "Lestrade –all that stuff. I'll enjoy seeing you do a bit of fancy sleuthing" in *Evil Under the Sun* (first published in 1941), again shows how much Christie is occupied by her most famous predecessor. So we are not surprised when Poirot uses his own set of tools to break into 'The Cheap Flat', although it's difficult to believe Holmes would use a small service lift. However, after telling Watson in 'Charles Augustus Milverton' that he feels he would have made "a highly efficient criminal" Holmes takes a leather case out of a drawer and opens it to reveal a number of instruments. He then says, "This is a first-class, up-to-date burgling kit, with nickel-plated jemmy, diamond-tipped glass-cutter, adaptable keys, and every modern improvement which the march of civilisation demands."

There are other subtle, and not so subtle, references to the Holmes canon in Christie's work. Hastings, like Watson in Baker Street, sometimes stands at the window of the lodging he shares with Poirot at the beginning of their acquaintance, and we have a sample of the sort of exchange which takes place between him and Poirot during the investigation into 'The Western Star'. Hastings begins by observing that a lady, richly dressed and wearing not only a fashionable hat but also magnificent furs, is not only coming slowly along the road outside but looking up at the houses as she goes. How, he asks, does Poirot deduce that she is coming to consult them? The little Belgian says it is simple. Their street is not aristocratic. There is no fashionable doctor, no fashionable dentist and no fashionable milliner. But there is a fashionable detective. An element of uncontrolled behaviour is obvious in the lady's progress. Poirot's client is a famous film star and is being closely followed by a motley crowd of admiring fans. This sense of 'madness' is echoed in the opening lines of Watson's account of 'The Beryl Coronet': "Holmes," said I, as I stood one morning in our bow window looking down the street, "here is a madman coming along. It seems rather sad that his relatives should allow him to come out alone." Unlike Poirot, Holmes rises from his chair, albeit lazily, looks over his friend's shoulder and rubs his hands together gleefully. He then says, "I believe he is coming here." Like the lady, the 'madman' is looking up at the numbers of the houses but, similarly to Hastings, Watson disputes whether or not Holmes really has a client. Both wrong, of course. But we've already seen how often the little Belgian sets his bigger and burlier helper to rights. Holmes says in answer to Watson's incredulous "Here?" "Yes; I rather think he is coming to consult me professionally. I think that I recognise the symptoms."

In 'A Case of Identity' Watson writes, "He had risen from his chair, and was standing between the parted blinds, gazing down into the dull neutral-tinted London street. Looking over his shoulder I saw that on the pavement opposite there stood a large woman with a a heavy fur boa round her neck, and a large curling red feather in a broad-brimmed hat which was tilted in a coquettish Duchess-of-Devonshire fashion over her ear. From under this great panoply she peeped up in a nervous, hesitating fashion at our windows, while her body oscillated backwards and forwards, and her fingers fidgeted with her glove buttons.

Suddenly, with a plunge as of the swimmer who leaves the bank, she hurried across the road, and we heard the sharp clang of the bell." Holmes has recognised the symptoms again and is fully prepared for her entrance.

Sherlock appears a little more subtly than this in the Christie canon when Hercule breathes heavily on a metal teapot and polishes it busily with a silk handkerchief ('The Disappearance of Mr. Davenheim'). Could it be an aid to detection, or used in the further mystification of Hastings? In *The Hound of the Baskervilles* Holmes deduces that Watson is inspecting a heavy walking stick (known as a Penang lawyer) even though he isn't looking at him and has been given no sign of his activity. Watson asks, "How did you know what I was doing? I believe you have eyes in the back of your head." To which Holmes replies, "I have at least a well-polished, silver-plated coffee-pot in front of me."

At some time Christie puts the following words into the mouth of her foil: "Now that war and the problems of war are things of the past I think I may safely venture to reveal to the world the part which my friend played in a moment of national crisis. The secret has been well guarded. Not a whisper of it has reached the press. But now that the need for secrecy has gone by I feel it is only just that England should know the debt it owes to my quaint little friend whose marvellous brain so ably averted a great catastrophe." Apart from the fact that he would never call Sherlock Holmes his "quaint little friend" this passage, from 'The Kidnapped Prime Minister', is pure Watson.

In *Death on the Nile* one of the characters says jeeringly, "Meditation on Death. Death the Recurring Decimal, by Hercule Poirot'. One of his well-known monographs." A word every Sherlock Holmes fan is familiar with since

Watson has told us all about them. Another jibe against the Great Detective occurs in *Lord Edgware Dies* when Brian Martin says to Poirot, "Not called in by Scotland Yard? No delicate matters to investigate for Royalty?"

"You confound fiction with reality, my friend," replies Poirot calmly, clearly suggesting he's real and Holmes is not. There are, however, other sly digs. Hastings, like Watson, wants action. Forgetting that Holmes often spends hours sitting in an armchair or on a pile of cushions on the floor thinking out the solutions to his various investigations, Poirot says he prefers to employ "the little grey cells" rather than crawl on his stomach like a fox. Both Hastings and Watson are frustrated when their respective detectives refuse to tell them anything. During the time that Hastings is waiting for a development in the sleuthing he says, "Poirot would talk only of extraneous things and refused to satisfy Japp's [and his] curiosity in the smallest degree." Holmes, as we know, tunes his fiddle or hides behind his pocket Petrarch when he wants to keep certain things up his sleeve.

Unlike the police, but very like Sherlock Holmes, Poirot is not officially in charge of an investigation. He has retired from the Belgian Force and, as with Holmes, only takes on cases that are of particular interest to him. But he, again like Holmes, works with the British police and shares his findings with them. He does this even when pursuing an independent line. It is Japp who makes the arrests and gets the credit, however. Something which Watson makes quite clear in his turn when he reports a conversation between Holmes and Lestrade at the successful conclusion of 'The Norwood Builder'. A grateful Lestrade says, "You have saved an innocent man's life, and you have prevented a very grave scandal, which would have ruined my reputation in the Force." To which Holmes replies, "Instead of being ruined, my good sir, you will find your reputation has been enormously advanced. Just make a few alterations in that report which you were writing, and they will understand how hard it is to throw dust into the eyes of Inspector Lestrade." The Scotland Yard man then asks, "And you won't want your name to appear?" To which the answer is, "Not at all. The work is its own reward."

There is a more than enough racism in Watson (and in the works of Agatha Christie) to match anyone's fear of foreign spies, etc. In the ludicrous tale 'The Yellow Face' the main villain of the story, as Mark Campbell remarks, is "the appalling racism of Victorian England." The old soldier ends the narrative on an optimistic note, but "the unconscious xenophobia of all (including, it must be said, the author) is particularly unsavoury." In 'The Three Gables' a huge Negro bursts into the room. He has been sent to intimidate 'Masser' Holmes and says he doesn't want "any lip" from him. Watson reports Holmes as saying, "It is certainly the last thing you need", and allows himself to remark on the visitor's "hideous mouth." Later Watson quotes Sherlock as saying, "I'm glad you didn't have to break his woolly head for him."

In *Lord Edgware Dies* Christie goes even further, making a character say (for no apparent reason except that he's drunk) "If we were a lot of chinks we wouldn't know each other apart" and "Anyway, I'm not a damned nigger." Jews also fare very badly, the inference being that their only real interest in life is money. "A sudden impish fancy flashed over me that if someone were really to offer Sir Montague a million pounds, old-world peace might go to the wall." Wealthy Jewish parents with marriageable daughters like to attract young men with prospects, even more so if these prospects include a title. "I am whispering cheerful nothings into the diamond encrusted ears of the fair (I beg her pardon, dark) Rachel in a box at Covent Garden. Her long Jewish nose is quivering with emotion."

In *Death in the Clouds* "The person who was usually regarded as M. Antoine himself, and whose real name was Andrew Leech and whose claims to foreign nationality consisted of having had a Jewish mother", speaks in broken English only when within the portals of his hairdressing salon. He is twice gratuitously referred to by one of his staff as 'Ikey Andrew' – which presumably chimed sufficiently enough with the prejudices of non-Jewish readers in the nineteen thirties not to stop them buying the book.

Holmes has his Baker Street irregulars, a bunch of street urchins able to glean useful facts and information for him from all over London. Poirot has Mr. Goby who, we are told in *After the Funeral*, is "famous for the acquiring of information. At the flick of [his] double jointed thumb hundreds of patient, questioning, plodding men and women, old and young, of all apparent stations in life, were despatched to question, and probe, and achieve results". These probing questioners are, socially, a cut above Holmes' little helpers. It wasn't always so, however. Here we have Mr. Goby again: "I've got what I could for you. I sent the boys out. They do what they can – good lads – good lads all of them, but not what they used to be in the old days. They don't come that way nowadays. Not willing to learn, that's what it is. They think they know everything, and they work to time. Shocking the way they work to time." In *Elephants Can Remember* Mr. Goby again performs miracles, providing information for Poirot while as usual addressing an item of furniture rather than his client. He has a small number of helpers, his 'legs' as he calls them, but "they aren't what they used to be." John Dickson Carr alludes to 'the deductive powers' of the Baker Street Irregulars but, as Watson relates it, the boys aren't detectives. They are, however, indefatigable in finding out what's wanted in order for Holmes to solve a crime – and never work to time. But the similarity between these young 'street arabs' and Mr. Goby's gang is nevertheless apparent.

Poirot in querulous mood complains that things are so quiet he will be reduced to finding lap dogs for old women. Holmes says in 'The Copper Beeches', "Man, or at least criminal man has lost all enterprise and originality. As to my own little practice, it seems to be degenerating into recovering lost lead pencils, and giving advice to young ladies from boarding-schools." The ever romantic Watson is in great hopes that this particular young lady will be of more than a passing interest to Holmes. He describes Miss Violet Hunter as "plainly but neatly dressed, with a bright, quick face, freckled like a plover's egg, and with the brisk manner of a woman who has had her own way to make in the world." Not quite the small, neat, clear-complexioned and admiring type he preferred, but eminently suited to Holmes. Alas, he was doomed to disappointment. True to form, his friend took no further interest in Violet once the case was over and she became the headmistress of a private school in Walsall – where, Watson remarks rather ruefully, "she has met with considerable success." Miss Hunter is no match in Holmes' mind for Irene Adler, who he habitually calls '*the* woman' in the same style as Poirot calls Countess Rossakoff "a woman in a thousand."

At the conclusion of *The Hound of the Baskervilles* Watson writes, "It was the end of November and Holmes and I sat, upon a raw and foggy night, on either side of a blazing fire in our sitting room in Baker Street." Hastings too sits in front of the fire with Poirot on more than one occasion in the lodgings they share (complete with housekeeper) before moving to more up-market accommodation in Whitehaven Mansions. A Poirot who can be less than kind – although not quite so savage as Holmes was in his remarks about Watson's choice of hiding place in 'The Solitary Cyclist'. In *'The Valley of Fear'* we have the following exchange between the two men, an exchange which seems even more savage, however:

"I am inclined to think," said I.
"I should do so," Sherlock Holmes remarked impatiently.

But on this occasion Watson hits back saying that, while he believed himself to be one of the most long-suffering of mortals, he was annoyed at the sardonic interruption. He even goes as far as to tell the detective how trying he can be at times. Sherlock, however, is too absorbed in his own thoughts to take immediate notice of what was, considering the provocation, a relatively mild reprimand. Less crude, but perhaps even more devastating, Holmes also says in *The Valley of Fear* "Your native shrewdness, my dear Watson, that innate cunning which is the delight of your friends, would surely prevent you from inclosing cipher and message in the same envelope."

The little Belgian says to Hastings, "I am pleased with you. You have a good memory and have given the facts faithfully. Of the order in which you present them I say nothing. Truly it is deplorable. But I make allowances. You are upset. Excuse me, *Mon Ami.* You dressed in haste and your tie is on one side. Permit me." He straightens the tie with "a deft gesture". But, as Anne Hart writes in *Agatha Christie's Poirot: The Life and Times of Hercule Poirot*, published by Pavilion Books in 1990, "What was being arranged here was Arthur Hastings' life, and there fell upon him not the mantle of Sherlock Holmes but of the loyal and credulous Doctor Watson."

APPENDIX

The officer who got back to England barely four months after the Battle of Maiwand was Surgeon-Major Alexander Francis Preston.

He had been badly wounded in the early stages of the fight and, although there were other surgeons in the field, is thought to be the model for Watson. Attached to the 66th Regiment of Foot – the Berkshires – he was, however, considerably older and more experienced than that relatively new recruit: who barely had time to become used to army life before being retired with a wound pension. Which, being of only nine months duration, was expected to tide him over while he looked for gainful employment in civilian life.

Preston, on the other hand, spent time 'at home' on half-pay for as long as it took for him to recover enough from his wounds to return to active service. His Service Record, which from what follows cannot be accepted as wholly reliable, states that he was wounded at Khush-ni-Nahud and a telegram sent to Headquarters to that effect. The same source says that he was again wounded in Kandahar less than a month later. If so, he was extremely unlucky; and it makes it difficult to believe he served throughout the siege of Kandahar which followed the British defeat. Preston was, however, Mentioned in Despatches. But the List of Commissioned Officers in the British Army merely states that he served in Afghanistan 1878-1880 and was wounded twice, without specifying where, geographically, his injuries were actually incurred. However, Leigh Maxwell (author of *My God-Maiwand!*) says that the Irishman was carried off the field, seriously wounded, early in the action.

Later, when an Enquiry into the Conduct of the Engagement was set up, every officer was required by The

Commander in Chief to write an account of the part he played in it. Preston's reads

After my wounds were attended to, I was lying quietly on my stretcher, when all of a sudden the bearers took it up and began running off with it as fast as they could go, shouting as they ran along that the ghazis were upon us. There was a regular stampede of men and animals making off at the best speed that they could. All was in utter confusion, no order of any kind, but everybody doing the utmost possible to save his own life and get out of the way of danger as fast and best as he could. With this object, all the loads had been taken off the baggage animals which were at once appropriated for riding purposes. The ground was, in consequence, covered with camp equipage, boxes of ammunition and treasure, mess-stores, wines and so on. My bearers had not gone far when they deserted me to a man; and after two other modes of conveyance in which I had been placed that afternoon had failed, I was finally taken up by a horse artillery wagon. All this time the stampede had been going on, and men of all races, horses, camels and bullocks passed in confusion.

During the retreat, the unfortunate Surgeon-Major in his horse artillery wagon had got as far as Ashu-Khan, about ten miles from Kandahar. Here the horses were unharnessed and watered. Whether or not they had had too much to drink, when they were returned to the wagon they appeared unable to move. Preston's narrative continues;

I lay helpless on the wagon for, I should say, a couple of hours expecting at every moment that some of our party would be shot as the villagers here, as they did all along

the road, kept continually firing at us. However, as a few stragglers of the 66th came up, I asked them to stay by me, and use their rifles in return. In this way the villagers were kept off. After some time, a camel with a pair of kajawas came up with Apothecary Cordiero of the Subordinate Medical Department (Bombay), who had been walking all night. He stopped the camel, and had me put in one of the kajawas, and regardless of his own safety remained with me for a long time and did everything in his power to assist me. I had not proceeded far in the kajawa before the cords holding it together commenced to give way, and to save me from falling the camel had to be made to lie down quickly. While lying helpless on the ground in the broken kajawa, I was passed by a large body of Sind Horse...After I had been lying on the ground for some time, Captain Slade of the RHA came up with one of his smooth-bore guns, and seeing me, and the situation I was in at once determined on endeavouring to save my life, and not to leave me to my inevitable fate. His horses were so utterly beaten that they would not have been equal to my additional weight; so in order to save my life he abandoned the gun and had me put upon the limber. Even then it was only by his splendid management and his presence of mind and great coolness in danger (for the inhabitants kept firing at us all along) that he succeeded in getting his horses to move at all[9]

A kajawa was a hybrid framework, part pannier and part stretcher, lashed on each side of a camel's hump. It would

---

[9] Reports and Narratives of the Officers who were Engaged at the Battle of Maiwand, 27th July 1880. Intelligence Branch, Army H.Q. India

have been less than comfortable for a fit man; but for a wounded man the rolling movement of the animal must have made it excruciating.

Preston was later (as a Returning Officer at Portsmouth) reprimanded for sending on troops inadequately provided for. But, unlike Dr. Watson, he recovered enough from his wounds to rejoin his corps and later served in China. It was at this juncture at Maiwand, however, that Gunner J. Hollis earned the Victoria Cross by running in front of the limber and drawing the Afghans' fire away from the gun carriage towards himself. He later left the army, joined the Bombay Police Force, committed bigamy and had the V.C. taken away from him 'For conduct likely to bring it into disrepute'. Many years later, George V changed the rules. He decreed that "A man should keep his medal even if he is on his way to the Scaffold."

Sgt. Mulvane of the Royal Horse Artillery was also at the Battle of Maiwand and earned the V.C. for rescuing a gunner – making him, like Hollis, a possible model for Watson's orderly, Murray. The Battleground was entirely in disarray and there were a large number of horses which had lost their riders and could be grabbed during the rout to carry away a wounded man.

Also From MX Publishing

The Sign of Fear

The first adventure of the 'female Sherlock Holmes'. A delightful fun adventure with your favourite supporting Holmes characters.

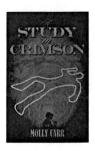

A Study in Crimson

The second adventure of the 'female Sherlock Holmes' with a host of sub-plots and new characters joining Watson and Fanshaw

The Chronology of Arthur Conan Doyle

The definitive chronology used by historians and libraries worldwide.

www.mxpublishing.com

Also from MX Publishing

Close To Holmes

A Look at the Connections Between Historical London, Sherlock Holmes and Sir Arthur Conan Doyle.

Eliminate The Impossible

An Examination of the World of Sherlock Holmes on Page and Screen.

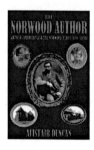

The Norwood Author

Arthur Conan Doyle and the Norwood Years (1891 - 1894)

www.mxpublishing.com

Also From MX Publishing

Arthur Conan Doyle, Sherlock Holmes and Devon

A Complete Tour Guide and Companion.

The Lost Stories of Sherlock Holmes

Eight more stories from the pen of John H Watson – compiled by Tony Reynolds.

www.mxpublishing.com

Also From MX Publishing

Watsons Afghan Adventure

Fascinating biography of Watson's time in Afghanistan from US Army veteran Kieran McMullen.

Shadowfall

Sherlock Holmes, ancient relics and demons and mystic characters. A supernatural Holmes pastiche.

Official Papers of The Hound of The Baskervilles

Very unusual collection of the original police papers from The Hound case.

www.mxpublishing.com

Also From MX Publishing

Aside Arthur Conan Doyle

A collection of twenty stories from ACD's close friend Bertram Fletcher Robinson.

Bertram Fletcher Robinson

The comprehensive biography of the assistant plot producer of The Hound of The Baskervilles

Wheels of Anarchy

Reprint and introduction to Max Pemberton's thriller from 100 years ago. One of the first spy thrillers of its kind.

www.mxpublishing.com

Also From MX Publishing

Bobbles and Plum

Four playlets from PG Wodehouse 'lost' for over 100 years – found and reprinted with an excellent commentary

The World of Vanity Fair

A specialist full-colour reproduction of key articles from Bertram Fletcher Robinson containing of colour caricatures from the early 1900s.

Tras Las He huellas de Arthur Conan Doyle (in Spanish)

Un viaje ilustrado por Devon.

www.mxpublishing.com

Also From MX Publishing

The Outstanding Mysteries of Sherlock Holmes

With thirteen Homes stories and illustrations Kelly re-creates the gas-lit, fog-enshrouded world of Victorian London

Rendezvous at The Populaire

Sherlock Holmes has retired, injured from an encounter with Moriarty. He's tempted out of retirement for an epic battle with the Phantom of the opera.

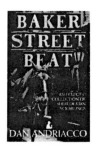

Baker Street Beat

An eclectic collection of articles, essays, radio plays and 'general scribblings' about Sherlock Holmes from Dr.Dan Andriacco.

www.mxpublishing.com
Also From MX Publishing

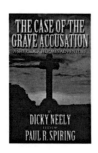

The Case of The Grave Accusation

The creator of Sherlock Holmes has been accused of murder. Only Holmes and Watson can stop the destruction of the Holmes legacy.

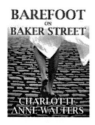

Barefoot on Baker Street

Epic novel of the life of a Victorian workhouse orphan featuring Sherlock Holmes and Moriarty.

Case of Witchcraft

A tale of witchcraft in the Northern Isles, in which some long-concealed secrets are revealed including about the Great Detective himself.

www.mxpublishing.com

221